Easton glanced at
snapped back on

The moment had been fleeting, but she'd caught something in that eye contact—something deep and warm.

"So you had a crush," she said, trying to sound normal. She still sounded breathy to her own ears. Bobbie started to whimper in the backseat, and Nora reached over to pop her pacifier back into her mouth.

"It was a weird thing to bond over," Easton admitted. "But I was the one guy who thought you were just as amazing as your dad did."

"I kind of knew you had a crush," she admitted.

"It was more."

Nora's heart sped up. She cast about for something to say but couldn't come up with anything. More than a crush... What was that? Love?

Dear Reader,

I'm a daddy's girl, and I married a man exactly like my father. They're both very techy, and they have similar quiet personalities that cover some very big opinions. My dad adored my mom, so when I met my husband and saw him loving me the same way I saw with my parents, I knew everything would be okay.

But what happens if your parents didn't have the kind of relationship that you want for yourself? That is where this book began—with a simple question: What would I do if I found out my dad had cheated on my mom? And what would that do to me? I confess, I don't think I'd deal with it gracefully.

I hope you enjoy reading this book as much as I enjoyed writing it. If you'd like to connect with me, you can find me on Facebook or on my blog, patriciajohnsromance.com. I'd love to see you!

Patricia Johns

THE TRIPLETS' COWBOY DADDY

Patricia Johns

Recycling programs
for this product may
not exist in your area.

ISBN-13: 978-0-373-75755-8

The Triplets' Cowboy Daddy

HARLEQUIN®
™ www.Harlequin.com

Printed in U.S.A.

Patricia Johns has an honors BA in English literature. She lives in Alberta, Canada, with her husband and son, where she writes full-time. Her first Harlequin novel came out in 2013, and you can find her books in the Love Inspired, Harlequin Western Romance and Harlequin Heartwarming lines.

Books by Patricia Johns

Harlequin Western Romance

Hope, Montana

Safe in the Lawman's Arms
Her Stubborn Cowboy
The Cowboy's Christmas Bride
The Cowboy's Valentine Bride

Love Inspired

His Unexpected Family
The Rancher's City Girl
A Firefighter's Promise
The Lawman's Surprise Family

Harlequin Heartwarming

A Baxter's Redemption

Visit the Author Profile page
at Harlequin.com for more titles.

To my husband and our son.
You are the best choices I ever made.
I love you!

Chapter One

Nora Carpenter could have cared for one baby easily enough. She could somehow have juggled two. But three—she'd never imagined that accepting the role of godmother to her half sister's babies would actually put her into the position of raising those babies on her own. She was still in shock.

Nora stood in her mother's brilliantly clean farmhouse kitchen, more overwhelmed than she had ever felt in her life. The three infants were still in their car seats, eyes scrunched shut and mouths open in hiccoughing wails. She stood over them, her jeans already stained from spilled formula and her tank top stretched from…she wasn't even sure what. She unbuckled the first infant—Rosie—and scooped her up. Rosie's cries subsided as she wriggled up against Nora's neck, but anxiety still made Nora's heart race as she fumbled with Riley's buckle. She'd come back to Hope, Montana, that afternoon so that her mother could help her out, but even that was more complicated than anyone guessed. These babies weren't just orphans in need of care; they were three tiny reminders that Nora's father hadn't been the man they all believed him to be.

Everything had changed—everything but this kitchen. The counters were crumb-free, as they always were, and the room smelled comfortingly, and very faintly, of bleach. Hand-embroidered kitchen towels hung from the stove handle—two of them, one with Monday sewn across the bottom, and one with Thursday. Today was Friday. Unless Dina Carpenter was making jam or doing canning, this was the natural state—immaculate, with no care for properly labeled towels. The babies' cries echoed through the house.

Rosie, Riley and Roberta had finished their bottles just before Nora's mother had left for a quick trip to the store for some baby supplies.

"I'll be fine!" Nora had said. Famous last words. The minute the door shut, the cries had begun, and no amount of cooing or rocking of car seats made a bit of difference.

There was a knock on the back door, and Nora shouted, "Come in!" as she scooped up Riley in her other arm and cuddled both babies close. Riley's cries stopped almost immediately, too, and that left Roberta—Bobbie, as Nora had nicknamed her—still crying in her car seat, hands balled up into tiny fists.

Nora had no idea who was at the door, and she didn't care. Whoever walked through that door was about to be put to work. Served them right for dropping by.

"Need a hand?" The voice behind her was deep—and familiar. Nora turned to see Easton Ross, the family's ranch manager, standing in the open door. He wore jeans and cowboy boots, his shirt pushed up his forearms to reveal ropy muscle. He'd changed a lot since their school days. Back then he'd been a skinny kid, perpetually shorter than she was. Not anymore. He was most definitely a grown man…and she was no longer the one with all the power. When her father died a few months ago, he'd left Easton a piece of property.

"Easton." She smiled tiredly. "Would you mind picking up Bobbie there? She needs a cuddle."

Her personal grudge against the man would have to wait.

"Yeah…okay…" He didn't sound certain, but he crossed the room and squatted in front of the car seat.

"You know how to pick up babies, don't you?" she asked.

"Uh…sort of." His face had hardened, his jawline now strong and masculine. He used to have acne as a teenager, but there was no sign of it now. Looking at him squatting there, she realized that she'd missed him more than she'd realized—and that wasn't just the fact that she didn't have enough hands right now. And yet, while she'd been away in the city, he'd been here with her dad, building a relationship that her father would reward him with her great-grandparents' homestead. Bile rose every time she thought about it.

"Support the head and the bottom," she instructed. "The rest will take care of itself."

Easton undid the buckle then cautiously scooped up the baby in his broad, calloused hands. Bobbie settled instantly as Easton pulled her against his chest. He looked down at the baby and then up at Nora.

"There," he said. "That worked."

"Thanks…" Nora heaved a sigh. The quiet was more than welcome.

"Bobbie?" he asked. The babies were all in pink sleepers.

"Her full name is Roberta. But she's my little Bobbie. It suits her."

Nora had only had the babies in her charge for a few days of her twelve-week parental leave from work, but she was already attached. They were so sweet, and so different from each other. Rosie was the quietest of the three, and Riley couldn't abide a wet diaper. Bobbie seemed to have the strongest personality, though, and Nora could already imagine their sisterly dynamic as they grew.

"Yeah, I guess so," he said. "Hi."

"Hi." She gave him a tight smile. "Nice to see you again."

Last time she saw him was at the reading of the will. She pushed back the unpleasant memory. Regardless, Easton was a fixture around here. They used to be good friends when they were younger, and they'd spent hours riding together, or just sitting on a fence and talking. When times were tough, Easton always seemed to materialize, and his solid presence made a difference. Apparently, her father had had equally warm memories.

Easton met her gaze, dark eyes softened by a smile. "You look good."

"Babies suit me, do they?" she joked.

"So the word around town—it's true, then?" he asked.

There it was—the beginning of the town's questions. There would be a lot of them, and the answers were complicated.

"What did you hear?" she asked warily. "How much do people know?"

"That you came back to town with triplets," he said. "That your dad had an affair, and you had a half sister…" He winced. "It that part true? I find it hard to believe of him. I knew your dad better than most—"

She chafed at that reminder. The homestead was an old farmhouse her great-grandparents had built with their own hands. Over the years, the Carpenters had maintained it and Nora's parents had used it as a guesthouse. It mattered, that old house. It was Nora's connection to her family's past and she'd loved that old place. For her father to have left it to someone else… that had stung. She only found out that he'd changed his will when he died. Her mother had been surprised because she said they'd talked about doing something for Easton, but hadn't landed on what exactly. Normally Cliff and Dina talked through everything. But it looked like even Easton had been in the dark about her father's biggest secret.

"Yes, it's true." Easton wouldn't be the only one to be disappointed in this town. "My half sister, Mia, introduced herself a couple of months ago. Her mom—the other woman—" those words tasted bitter "—passed away a few years ago, and Mia was looking for her dad's side of the family. When I met her, she was already pregnant. There was no dad—she'd gone to a sperm bank. She really wanted kids and hadn't met the right guy yet."

Mia had had no idea about the affair and she never got a chance to meet Cliff. She had introduced herself after he died. It had been an awkward meeting, but Nora and Mia had recognized something in each other. Maybe they felt the genetic link. They'd both been raised only children, and to find a sibling was like a childhood daydream come true. Except this was real life, and they'd both had to come to terms with their father's infidelity.

"And you're godmother," Easton concluded.

"Yes. When she asked me to be godmother, I swear, I thought it was just a kind gesture. I never imagined this…"

Mia had died from childbirth complications—triplets being a high risk pregnancy to begin with—and Nora had grieved more deeply than she thought possible for a sister she'd only known a couple of months, whose existence rocked her own world. Nora was certain they'd have been close.

"Wow." Easton cleared his throat. "So your mom… I mean, these babies…"

"Yes, these babies are my father's illegitimate grandchildren." Nora sighed. "And Mom isn't taking it well."

That was an understatement. Nora hadn't told her mother, Dina, about Mia for a few weeks, afraid of causing her mother more grief than she was already shouldering since her husband's death. So Dina Carpenter hadn't had long to adjust to this new information before Nora and the babies arrived on her doorstep.

And Dina *hadn't* adjusted. She was still coming to terms with her late husband's infidelity and learning to run the ranch on her own. The babies only seemed to fuel more heartbreak.

"So what are you going to do?" Easton asked.

Footsteps sounded on the wooden staircase outside; then the door opened and Dina came inside, dropping some shopping bags on the floor. She was plump, with graying blond hair pulled back into a ponytail. She shut the door behind her then looked up.

"You're back," Nora said.

"I got some baby clothes, diapers, formula, soothers, three bouncy chairs—they might help with..." Dina's voice trailed off. "Hi, Easton."

Nora recognized the trepidation in her mother's voice. The secret was out. She'd been holding this one close to her chest, and Nora knew how much her mother dreaded the whole town knowing the ugly truth about her husband's affair. So did Nora, for that matter. It was worse somehow that her father wasn't here to answer any questions, or take the brunt of this for them. He deserved to feel ashamed; they didn't. Nora and her mother hadn't been the ones to betray trust; he had. But he was dead, and they were left with the fallout of Cliff Carpenter's poor choices.

"Hi, Mrs. Carpenter." Easton stood awkwardly, the baby nestled against his chest, and seemed almost afraid to move. "Just lending a hand. I came by to tell you that we're rotating pastures for fence maintenance, and that will require a bit of overtime from the ranch hands."

"More overtime?" Dina sighed. "No, no, do it. The southwest fences, right? We put them off last year, so…" She sighed. "Is that all?"

"Yeah." Easton nodded. "I can get going." He looked down at the baby in his arms then at Dina as if he didn't know what to do.

If the homestead was still in the family, Nora would have moved in there with the babies to give her mother some space, but that was no longer an option. Nora and Dina would just have to deal with this together.

"I guess we'll have to get the babies settled in your old bedroom," Dina said. She paused, put a hand over her eyes. "I still can't believe it's come to this."

"Mom, you know I can't take care of them alone—"

"And why did you agree to be godmother?" Her mother heaved a sigh. "I swear, your generation doesn't think!" She pressed her lips together. "I'm sorry, Nora. What's done is done."

Dina grabbed the bags and headed down the hallway toward Nora's old bedroom. Nora and Easton exchanged a look.

"She's not taking this well," Nora said, feeling like she had to explain somehow.

"I can see that." Easton glanced in the direction his boss had disappeared. "You going to be okay here?"

"Do I have a choice?" Nora failed to keep the chill from her tone. The guesthouse would have been the perfect solution, but Easton owned it now. That wouldn't be lost on him. No matter how big the ranch house, the five of them would be cramped. Her mother was right—she hadn't thought this through. If she'd imagined that she'd ever have to step in and raise these girls, she would have found a polite way to decline the honor. Mia must have had some close friends…maybe some relative on her mother's side that she could have named as godparent.

Dina came back into the kitchen, her eyes redder than before. Had her mother been crying in the other room?

"Okay, let's figure this out," Dina said, her voice wooden. "Where are they going to sleep?"

NORA WAS STARING BLANKLY, and she looked like she wanted to cry. Two of the babies were snuggled in her arms. It was a stupid time for Easton to be noticing, but she was just as gorgeous as she'd always been, with her honey-blond hair and long, slim legs. He'd been halfway in love with her since the sixth grade. She'd never returned his feelings—ever.

Bobbie took a deep breath in her sleep then scrunched her face. He felt a surge of panic and patted the little rump as if soothing the baby would fix all of this. He glanced toward the car seat then at Bobbie. He wanted out of here—to get some space of his own to think this through. Except Nora and Dina looked like they were ready to collapse into tears, and here he stood, the legal owner of the obvious solution.

Easton was a private man. He liked quiet and solitude, and he had that with his new home—Cliff had known exactly how much it would mean to him. But Cliff hadn't known that he'd have three granddaughters landing on his doorstep after his death…

Dina obviously needed some time to process all this, and Nora needed help—he could feel her desperation emanating from her like waves…

Guilt crept up inside him—a nagging certainty that he stood between Nora and her solution. He didn't want to go back to the way things were when they were teens, and he certainly didn't want to give up that house and land that his boss had given him, but he couldn't just stand here and watch them scramble for some sort of arrangement as if it didn't affect him, either. He felt responsible.

The words were coming out of his mouth before he had a chance to think better of them. "You can stay with me, Nora. It's not a problem."

Nora and Dina turned toward him, relief mingled with guilt written all over both faces. There had always been tension between mother and daughter, and the current situation hadn't improved things.

"You sure?" Nora asked.

"You bet. It'll be fine. There's lots of room. Just for a few days, until you and your mom figure this out." He was making this sound like a weekend away, not a complete invasion of his privacy, but he was already entangled in this family and had been for years. This was for old time's sake—for the friendship that used to mean so much to him. And maybe this was also a guilt offering for having inherited that house to begin with.

The next few minutes were spent gathering up baby supplies and getting the car seats back into Nora's four-door pickup truck. As Nora got into the driver's seat, Dina visibly deflated from where she stood at the side door. She'd been holding herself together for her daughter's sake, it seemed, and she suddenly looked small and older.

Cliff may have been many things, but he had been a good man at heart, and no one would convince Easton otherwise. A good husband? Perhaps not, given the recent revelation. But a man could be good at heart and lousy with relationships. At least Easton hoped so, because he seemed to fall into that category himself. If it weren't for Cliff, Easton's life would have turned out a whole lot differently. Loyalty might be in short supply, but Easton knew where his lay.

He got into his own rusted-out Ford and followed Nora down the familiar drive toward his little house. *His* house. Should he feel so territorial about the old place? He'd fixed it up a fair amount since taking ownership, and the work had brought him a lot of comfort. He'd grown up in a drafty old house in town filled with his dad's beer bottles and piles of dishes that never got washed. So when he found out that Cliff had left him the house and the land, something inside him had grown—like roots sinking down, giving more security than he'd ever had. He'd stared at that deed, awash in gratefulness. He'd never been a guy who let his feelings show, but he had no shame in the tears that misted his eyes when he shook the lawyer's hand.

I shouldn't have gotten attached. And that was the story of his life, learning not to get attached, because nothing really lasted.

The farmhouse was a small, two-story house with white wooden siding and a broad, covered front porch.

He hadn't been expecting company when he'd headed out for his morning chores, and he hoped that he'd left it decently clean. But this was his home, and while the situation was emotionally complicated, the legalities wouldn't change. Mr. Carpenter had left it to him. The deed was in a safety deposit box at the bank.

After they'd parked, Easton hopped out of his truck and angled around to her vehicle, where she was already unbuckling car seats.

"Thanks," Nora said as she passed him the first baby in her seat. "I don't know how to balance three of them yet. I should probably call up Mackenzie Granger and see if she has any ideas. She's got the twins, after all."

He held the front door open for her with the heel of his boot and waited while she stepped inside. The sun was lowering in the sky, illuminating the simple interior. Nora paused as she looked around.

"It's different than I left it."

"Yeah..." He wasn't sure how apologetic he should be here. "I got rid of the old furniture. It was pretty musty."

Easton hadn't put anything on the walls yet. He had a few pictures of his mother, but they didn't belong on the wall. She'd run off when he was eight—left a letter stuck to the fridge saying she couldn't handle it anymore, and that Easton was now his father's problem. He'd never seen her again. Considering the only family pictures he had were a few snapshots of his mom, the walls had stayed bare.

"Why did my dad leave this house to you?" Nora

turned to face him. "I can't figure that part out. Why would he do that?"

Easton hadn't been the one to hurt her, but he was the one standing in front of her, regardless, and he felt an irrational wave of guilt. He was caught up in her pain, whether he meant to be or not.

"I don't know…" It had been a kind gesture—more than kind—and he'd wondered ever since if there were hidden strings. "A while ago, he said that he needed someone to take care of it, put some new life into it. I'd assumed that he wanted to rent it out or something. I didn't expect this."

"But this is my great-grandparents' home," she said. "I loved this place…"

She had… He remembered helping the family paint the old house one year when he was a teenager, and Nora had put fresh curtains in the windows in the kitchen—she'd sewn them in home economics class. She did love this old house, but then she'd gone to college and gotten a city job, and he'd just figured she'd moved on.

"You had your own life in the city. Maybe your dad thought—"

"That doesn't mean I don't have roots here in Hope!" she shot back. "This house is mine. It should have been mine… My father should *never* have done this." She had to point her anger at someone, and it was hard to tell off the dead.

"What he should have done is debatable," Easton said. "But he made a choice."

She didn't answer him, and he didn't expect her to.

She hated this, but he couldn't change facts, and he wasn't about to be pushed around, either. They'd just have to try to sort out a truce over the next few days.

"I'm making some tea," he added. "You want some?"

They'd been friends back in the day, but a lot had changed. Easton grew up and filled out. Nora had gone to college and moved to the city. He was now legal owner of a house she was still attached to, and an old friendship wasn't going to be cushion enough for all of this.

"Yes, tea would be nice." Her tone was tight.

"Nora." He turned on the rattling faucet to fill up the kettle. "I don't know what you think I did, but I never asked for this house. And I never angled for it."

"You didn't turn it down, either."

No, he hadn't. He could have refused the inheritance, but it had been an answer to midnight prayers, a way to step out from under his past. Mr. Carpenter's gift had made him feel more like family and less like the messed-up kid who needed a job. Mr. Carpenter had seen him differently, but he suspected Nora still saw him the same way she always had—a skinny kid who would do pretty much anything she asked to make her happy.

And as dumb as it was, he also saw her the same way he always had—the beautiful girl whom he wished could see past his flaws and down to his core. He was a man now—not a boy, and most certainly not a charity case. Nora was a reminder of a time he didn't want to revisit—when he'd been in love with a girl who took what he had to offer and never once saw him as more than a buddy. It hadn't been only her...he'd been an isolated kid looking for acceptance anywhere he could get it, and he didn't like those memories. They were marinated in loneliness.

That wasn't who he was anymore. Everything had changed around here. Including him.

Chapter Two

Easton heard the soft beep of an alarm go off through a fog of sleep, and he blinked his eyes open, glancing at the clock beside him. It was 3 a.m., and it wasn't his alarm. The sound filtered through the wall from the bedroom next door. He had another hour before he had to be up for chores, and he was about to roll over when he heard the sound of footsteps going down the staircase.

Nora was up—though the babies were silent. It was strange to have her back...to have her here. She'd stayed away, made a life in the city where she had an office job of some sort. She would come back for a weekend home every now and then, but she'd spent her time with friends, cousins, aunts and uncles. Easton didn't fit into any category—not anymore. He was an employee. He'd worked his shifts, managed the ranch hands and if he got so much as a passing wave from her, he'd be lucky.

Now she was in his home. Her presence seemed to be a constant reminder of his status around here—employee. Even this house—legally his—felt less like his own. There was something about Nora Carpenter that put him right back into his place. For a while he'd been able to forget about his status around here, believe he could be more, but with her back—

He wasn't going to be able to sleep listening to the soft sounds of a woman moving around the house anyway. He swung his legs over the side of his bed, yawning. The footsteps came back up the narrow staircase again, and he rose to his feet, stretching as he did. He was in a white T-shirt and pajama bottoms, decent enough to see her. He crossed his bedroom and opened the door.

Nora stood in the hallway, three bottles of milk in her hands, and she froze at the sight of him. Her blond hair tumbled over her shoulders, and she stood there in a pair of pajamas—a tank top and pink, pin-striped cotton shorts.

She's cute.

She always had been, and no matter how distant or uninterested she got, he'd never stopped noticing.

"Sorry," she whispered. "I was trying to be quiet."

He hadn't actually been prepared to see her like this—her milky skin glowing in the dim light from her open bedroom door, her luminous eyes fixed on him apologetically. She was stunning, just as she'd always been, but she was more womanly now—rounder, softer, more sure of herself. They should both be sleeping right now, oblivious to each other. That was safer by far.

"The babies aren't crying," he pointed out.

"I'm following the advice of the social worker who gave me the lowdown on caring for triplets. She said to feed them on a schedule. If I wait for them to wake up, we'll have three crying babies."

It made sense, actually. He'd never given infant care—let alone infant care for triplets—much thought before. He should leave her to it, go back to bed... maybe go downstairs and start breakfast if he really couldn't sleep.

"Need a hand?" he asked.

Where had that come from? Childcare wasn't his domain, and frankly, neither was Nora. He'd been through this before with her—he knew how it went. She batted her eyes in his general direction, he got attached, she waltzed off once her problems were solved, and he was left behind, wrung out. Letting her stay here was help enough. As was picking up the crib for the babies after he brought her to the house. He couldn't be accused of callous indifference, but he also couldn't go down that path again.

She smiled at his offer of help. "I wouldn't turn it down."

Well, that took care of that. He trailed after her into the bedroom. The crib sat on one side of the room, Nora's rumpled bed on the other side. A window, cracked open, was between the two, and a cool night breeze curled through the room. The babies lay side by side along the mattress of the crib. Rosie and Riley looked pretty similar to his untrained eye, but he could pick out Bobbie. She was considerably bigger than the other two. But "big" was relative; they were all pretty tiny.

"I was hoping my mom would be able to help me with this stuff," Nora said as she picked up the first baby and passed her to him along with a bottle. "That's Rosie," she added.

She proceeded to pick up the other two and brought them to her unmade bed, where she propped them both up against her pillow. She wiggled the bottle nipples between their lips.

"Time to eat," she murmured.

The babies started to suck without any further prompting, and Easton looked down at the infant in his arms. He followed Nora's lead, teasing the bottle into Rosie's tiny mouth, and she immediately began to drink. It felt oddly satisfying.

"So this is how it's done," he said with a soft laugh.

"Apparently," Nora replied.

They were both silent for a few moments, the only sound babies slurping. He leaned an elbow against the crib, watching the tiny bubbles move up the bottle and turn into froth at the top of the milk. He'd done this with calves on a regular basis, but never with a baby.

"I don't blame your mom," Easton said.

"Me, neither," she replied quietly. "I just didn't know where else to go. When you feel lost, you find your mom."

Easton had never had that pleasure. His mom had abandoned them, and his dad...well, his dad could barely keep his own life together, let alone help Easton.

"Sorry..." She winced. "I forgot."

Yeah, yeah, his pathetic excuse for a family. Poor Easton. He was tired of that—the pity, the charitable thoughts. *Be thankful for what you have, because someone else thinks you're lucky.* It was a deep thought for the privileged as they considered how bad they could truly have it, before they breathed a sigh of relief that they still retained their good fortune.

"So why didn't you come back more often?" Easton asked, changing the subject.

"I was busy." She shot him a sidelong look. "Why?"

"It just seems to me that two weekends a year isn't much time with your family."

"We talked on the phone. What's it to you?"

He'd struck a nerve there, but she had a point. Who was he to lecture her about family bonds? He didn't have any of his own that counted for much. Besides, his complaint wasn't really about how much time she spent with her family. He'd missed her, too. His life kept going in Hope, Montana, and hers had moved on in the wider world. He resented her for that—for forgetting him.

"Mom and I—" Nora sighed. "We locked horns a lot."

"Yeah…" He hadn't expected her to open up. "I noticed it, but I never knew what it was about."

"Everything." She shook her head. "Politics, religion, current events…you name it, we land on opposite sides of it. When I left for college, it gave me a whole new freedom to be me, without arguing with Mom about it. So I stayed away a lot."

"Is that why you didn't tell her about your half sister?" he asked.

He was watching her as she sat on her bed facing the babies, one leg tucked under herself. Bobbie finished her bottle first, and Nora put it down, still feeding Riley with the other hand. She was oddly coordinated as she bottle-fed two infants. Maybe it came from bottle-feeding orphaned farm animals. If you could wrangle a lamb or a calf into taking a bottle, maybe it was a skill like riding a bike.

"I needed to sort it all out in my own head before I told her about it," Nora said, oblivious to his scrutiny. "It was like anything else. I thought I could have a sister—some semblance of a relationship with her—but I was pretty sure Mom would see that as a betrayal."

"I get it."

In fact, he understood both sides of it. It had to be hard for Dina to see her one and only daughter bonding with her late husband's love child. Yet he could understand Nora's desire to know her sister. The whole situation was a painful one—the sort of thing that made him mildly grateful for his lack of family coziness. At least he couldn't be let down any more than he already had been. Rock bottom was safe—there was no farther to fall.

Rosie was almost finished with her bottle, but she'd stopped drinking. He pulled it out of her mouth, leaving a little trail of milk dribbling down her chin.

"Is she done?" Nora asked.

"She stopped drinking." He held up the bottle.

"Okay. Just burp her, then."

Burp the baby. Of course. He knew the concept here—he wasn't a Neanderthal. He lifted Rosie to his shoulder, and she squirmed in her sleep, letting out a soft cry. Great, now he'd done it.

"Just pat her back," Nora said.

Easton gently tapped Rosie's back and she burped almost immediately, leaving a warm, wet sensation on his shoulder, dripping down toward his chest. He cranked his head to the side and could just make out the mess.

Nora chuckled. "Sorry."

Riley had finished her bottle, and Nora reached for Bobbie. It was an odd sort of assembly line as she burped them and he laid them back in the crib. He pulled the white T-shirt off over his head, getting the wet material away from his skin. He wadded up the shirt and gave his shoulder an extra scrub. It was then that he realized he was standing in front of Nora shirtless. Her gaze flickered over his muscular chest, and color rose in her cheeks.

"I'll just—" He pointed toward the door. He needed to get out of there. He'd fed and burped a baby—mission accomplished. He wasn't supposed to be hanging out with her, and he definitely wasn't supposed to be this casual with her, either.

"Okay. Sure—"

Nora's gaze moved over his torso once more, then she looked away quickly. She was uncomfortable, too. Soiled T-shirt in hand, he headed out of the room. That hadn't been the plan at all, and he felt stupid for not thinking ahead. Who knew what she thought now—that he was hitting on her, maybe? That couldn't be further from the truth.

Blast it, he was up now. He might as well go down and make some breakfast. An early start was better than a late one.

NORA HADN'T EVER seen Easton Ross looking quite so grown-up. And she hadn't imagined that under that shirt were defined muscles and a deep tan. He had a six-pack—that had been hard to miss—and it left her a little embarrassed, too. A good-looking man might be easy enough to appreciate in a picture or on TV, but when he stood in your bedroom in the moonlight... She laid Bobbie next to Riley and Rosie in the crib and looked down at them for a moment, watching the soft rise and fall of their tiny chests.

It wasn't because she'd never seen a man without a shirt before. She'd always had a pretty healthy romantic life. But this was Easton—an old buddy, a quiet guy in the background. If he'd looked a little less impressive, she wouldn't have felt so flustered, but my goodness... When exactly had skinny, shy Easton turned into *that*?

She was awake now—she'd have to get used to going back to bed after the 3 a.m. feeding, but she could hear the soft clink of dishes downstairs, and she had a feeling that she and Easton needed to clear the air.

Grabbing a robe, Nora pulled it around herself and padded softly down the narrow, steep staircase. She paused at the bottom on a landing that separated the kitchen from the living room. Looking into the kitchen, she could see Easton at the stove, his back to her. He was in jeans and a fresh T-shirt now, his feet bare. The smell of percolating coffee filtered through the kitchen.

"Easton?" She stepped into the kitchen, tugging her robe a little tighter.

He turned, surprised. "Aren't you going to try to sleep some more?"

"I'm not used to the up and down thing yet. When I get tired enough, I'm sure I will."

He nodded and turned back to the pan. "You want breakfast?"

"Kind of early," she said with a small smile.

"Suit yourself." He dropped several strips of bacon into the pan.

"Look," she said, pulling out a kitchen chair with a scrape and sitting down. "I think I'm in the way here."

"Since when?"

"Since I woke you up at 3 a.m."

"I'll be fine." His tone was gruff and not exactly comforting. Was he doing this because she was the boss's daughter? It had to factor in somewhere.

"This is your home, Easton."

"You noticed." He cast her a wry smile then turned around fully, folding his arms across his chest. Yes, she had noticed. She didn't have to like it, but she was capable of facing facts.

"I should take the babies back to the house with my mom," she said. "I'm sorry. I hate that my dad left this place to you, but he did. So…"

She was sad about that—angry, even—but it wasn't Easton's fault. He could have turned it down, but who would turn down a house? She wouldn't have, either.

"You don't need to leave," he said.

"Oh." She'd thought he'd jump at any excuse to get her out of his home. If this night had proven anything, it was that this space was very much Easton's, and that felt awkward. This kitchen, where she remembered making cookies with her great-grandmother, was *his* kitchen now. She'd imagined she'd find peace here, but she'd been wrong. She shouldn't be surprised. A lot of her "perfect" memories hadn't been what she thought.

"You don't seem comfortable with me here, though," she countered. "And if I'm bound to make someone feel uncomfortable, it should be my own mother, don't you think?"

"I don't have a problem with you staying here," he replied, turning back to the pan. He flipped the bacon strips with a fork, his voice carrying over the sizzle. "Do you realize that I've worked on this land since I was fourteen?"

"Yeah. It's been a while."

"That's sixteen years. And over those years, you and I became friends."

"I know."

"Real friends." He turned back, his dark gaze drilling into hers. "Do you remember when you broke up with Kevin Price? We talked for hours about that. I was there for you. I was there for you for Nathan Anderson, Brian Neville... I was there to listen, to offer advice. I mean, my advice was always the same—pick a better guy—but I was there."

Easton *had* been there for her, and she felt a blush rise at the memories. One rainy, soggy autumn day, they'd sat in the hayloft together, talking about a guy who wasn't treating her right. They'd sat for hours, just talking and talking, and she'd opened up more in that evening than she had with any guy she'd dated. But then her father had found them, ordered Easton back to work and told Nora to get inside. She could still remember the stormy look on her father's face. He hadn't liked it—probably assumed more was happening in the hayloft than a conversation.

Nora had talked too much back then. It had just felt so nice to have someone who listened like he did, but she might have led him on a little bit. She was a teenage girl, and her emotional world was vast and deep—in her own opinion, at least. She was mildly embarrassed about that now, but she wasn't any different than other girls. Easton was just a part-time ranch hand, and a guy. He hadn't been quite so in touch with his own "vast and deep" emotional life, and maybe he'd been a little in awe of her…maybe he'd nursed a mild crush. But she hadn't ever considered him as more than a buddy.

"I was an idiot," she said with a short laugh.

"And then you picked up and left for college, and that was it."

Well, that sure skipped a lot—like all the college applications, the arguments with her mother about living on campus or off and all the rest of the drama that came with starting a new phase of life. And since when was college a problem?

She frowned. "I went to college. You knew I was going."

"Thing is," he said, "you walked away, and life went on. For sixteen years I worked this land, drove the cattle, worked my way up. I'm ranch manager now because I know every job on this ranch and could do it myself if I had to. No one can get one over on me."

"You're good at what you do," she confirmed. "Dad always said so."

"And when you did come back to visit, you'd wave at me across the yard. That was it."

Admittedly, their relationship changed over the years. But having him here—that was the awkward part. If they'd just been school friends, then a change in the closeness they shared would have been natural—like the ebb and flow of any relationship. But he'd worked with her father, so unlike her school friends—where some of those old friendships could die a quiet death— she still saw Easton on a regular basis. From a distance, at least. He couldn't just slide into the past. When she did come home, she only had a few days, and she had to see a lot of people in that time.

"I was busy," she replied. "Friends and family—"

She heard it as it came out of her mouth. Friends— and she hadn't meant him. She'd meant people like Kaitlyn Mason, who she'd been close with since kin- dergarten. She winced. There was no recovering from that one, but it didn't make it any less true. Easton hadn't been high enough on her list of priorities when she'd come back.

"Yeah," he said with a sad smile. "Anyway, I was the worker, you were the daughter. Well, your dad saw fit to give me a little patch of land. I *worked* for this. I know that your great-grandparents built this house, and I know it means a whole lot to you, but I'm not about to sell it or tear it down. I actually think I might take your dad's advice."

"Which was?" she asked.

"To get married, have a few kids."

That had been her father's advice to him? Her father's advice to her had always been "Wait a while. No rush. Get your education and see the world." The double standard there irritated her, but she couldn't put her finger on why. Whoever Easton decided to marry and whatever kids they'd have, they'd be no kin of the people who built this house with their own hands. Her family—the Carpenters—had been born here, had died here… Easton might have worked for her father, but he didn't *deserve* this house.

"Anyone special in mind?" she asked, trying to force a smile.

"Nope."

There was no use arguing. The house was his. She couldn't change it or fight it. Maybe one day she could convince him to sell to her, but that was about as much as she could do.

"If you ever want to sell this house," she said, "come to me first."

He nodded. "Deal."

Easton turned back to the stove and lifted the bacon from the pan with his tongs, letting it drip for a moment in sizzling drops before he transferred it to a plate. She had to admit—it smelled amazing. He grabbed a couple of eggs and cracked them into the pan. Was that it? Was that all she could ask from him—to sell to her if he ever felt like it? Probably, and he didn't look like he was about to back down, either.

He'd had a point, though. He'd spent more time with her dad than she had…he'd know things.

"Did you know about the other woman?" Nora asked.

He grabbed a couple thick slices of bread, dumped

the bacon onto one of them, added the eggs sunny side up, and slapped the second piece on top. He turned toward her slowly and met her eyes.

"I get that you're mad at him," he said. "And you've got every right to be. But he wasn't my father, and what he did inside of marriage or outside of it wasn't my business."

Nora stared at him, shocked. Was that the kind of man Easton was? He was just talking about a marriage and family of his own. She'd thought he'd have a few more scruples than that.

"But did you know?" she demanded.

"I'm saying he was my boss," Easton retorted, fire flashing in his eyes. "His personal life wasn't my business. I had no idea about the other woman—how could I know? We were working cattle, not cozying up to women. I'm not going to bad-mouth him, even if that would make you feel better for a little while. He was good to me. He was honest and fair with me. He taught me everything I know and set me up with this house. If you're looking for someone to complain about him and pick him apart with, you'd better keep looking. I'm not that guy."

He dropped his plate on the table and squashed the sandwich down with the palm of his hand. Then he grabbed a few pieces of paper towel and wrapped it up.

"You're nothing if not loyal, Easton," she said bitterly. Loyal to the man who'd given him land. He should have been loyal to a few basic principles.

Easton tossed the wrapped sandwich into a plastic bread bag then headed to the mudroom.

"I'm sorry for what he did to you," he said, not raising his head as he plunged his feet into his boots. "I get that it was a betrayal. But I'm staff, and you're family. I know the line."

The line? What line? Was he mad that they'd grown apart over the years, that she'd moved away to Billings for a degree in accounting? What line was so precious that he couldn't stand up for the women who had been wronged?

"What does that mean?" she demanded. "Do you want me to go? Have I crossed a line with you?"

He grabbed his hat and dropped it on his head.

"No," he said quietly. "Stay."

He didn't look like he was going to expand upon that, and he pulled open the door, letting in a cool morning draft.

"You forgot your coffee," she said.

"I leave it on the stove to let it cool down a bit," he said. "I'll have it in an hour when I get back."

With that, he stepped outside into the predawn grayness. Then the door banged shut after him, leaving her alone with a freshly percolated pot of coffee and three sleeping babies.

Easton had made himself clear—his loyalty belonged to her dad. Well, her father had lost hers. Ironic, wasn't it, that the one person to stand by Cliff Carpenter's memory was the hired hand?

Chapter Three

Around midmorning, Nora heard a truck rumble to a stop outside the house. She looked out the window to see her mother hop out of the cab. She was wearing a pair of fitted jeans and boots, and when she saw Nora in the window, she waved. Nora hadn't realized how much she'd missed her mom until she saw her, then she felt a wave of relief. It reminded her of waiting to be picked up at Hope Elementary School. All the other kids got on the bus, and Nora had to sit on the curb, alone. Her heart would speed up with a strange joy when she finally saw her mom in the family truck. She felt that joy on that school curb for the same reason: sometimes a girl—no matter the age—just needed her mom's support.

The babies were all sleeping in their bouncy chairs, diapers changed and tummies full. Nora's ridiculously early morning was already feeling like a mistake. She was exhausted. Back in the city, she'd been working in the accounting office for a company that produced equestrian gear. She'd worked hard, put in overtime, but she'd never felt weariness quite like this. A work friend had told her that her twelve weeks of parental leave would be more work than the office, but she hadn't believed it until now.

Nora pulled open the side door and ambled out into the warm August sunshine.

"Morning," she called.

"Mackenzie Granger dropped this by," her mother said, pulling a collapsed stroller out of the bed of the truck. "She said she got the triplet stroller for the boys and the new baby, but hasn't used it as much as she thought she would."

Nora couldn't help the smile that came to her face. She'd been wondering how she'd ever leave the house again with three infants, but thank God for neighbors with twin toddlers and new babies.

"I'll have to call her and thank her," Nora said. "And thank you for bringing it by."

Her mother carried the stroller over and together they unfolded it and snapped it into its open position. It was an umbrella stroller with three seats lined up side by side. It was perfect. Not too big, not too heavy, and she could transport all three babies at once.

"I had an idea." Dina shot Nora a smile. "Let's load the babies into this and you can come pick the last of the strawberries with me."

They used to pick strawberries together every summer when Nora was young. They'd eat as they picked, and even with all the eating, they'd fill bucket after bucket. Dina would make jam with some of them, freeze a bunch more and then there would be fresh strawberries for everything from waffles to ice cream.

Nora used to love strawberry-picking. Then she became a teenager, and she and her mother stopped getting along quite so well.

Nora met her mother's gaze, and she saw hope in Dina's eyes—the flimsy, vulnerable kind of hope that wavered, ready to evaporate. Maybe her mother was thinking of those sweet days, too, when they used to laugh together and Dina would let Nora whip up some cream for the berries.

"Yeah, okay," Nora said.

They transferred the babies to the stroller quickly enough, and the stroller rattled and jerked as Nora pushed it down the gravel road—the babies undisturbed. Maybe this was why Mack hadn't used it much. The wheels were quite small, so every rock could be felt underneath them. But Nora had gotten them all outside, and that was a feat in itself.

"So what are you going to do about the babies?" her mother asked as they walked.

"Would it be crazy to raise them?" Nora asked.

"Three infants on your own?" her mother asked.

"Three infants, you and me."

Her mother didn't answer right away, and sadness welled up inside Nora. It *was* crazy. And it was too much to ask of her mom right now. Maybe ever. Her mother reached over and put a hand on top of Nora's on the stroller handle.

"I've missed you," Dina said quietly. "It's nice to have you home."

It wasn't an answer—not directly, at least—but it was clear enough. They were still on opposite sides, it seemed, even with the babies. But Nora had always been stubborn, and she wasn't willing to let this go gracefully.

"I came home because I thought you'd help me," Nora pressed.

"And I will. As much as I can."

They all had limits to what they could give, and Nora had taken on more than she could possibly handle on her own. The problem was that she was already falling in love with these little girls. With every bottle, every diaper change, every snuggle and coo and cry, her heart was becoming more and more entwined with theirs. But was keeping them the right choice?

The strawberry patch was on the far side of the main house, and Nora parked the stroller in the shade of an apple tree then moved into the sunshine where Dina had the buckets waiting. Dina came back over to the stroller and squatted down in front of it. Sadness welled in her eyes as she looked at the sleeping infants.

"I get it," Dina said, glancing up at her daughter. "When I first held you, I fell in love, too. It couldn't be helped."

"They're sweet," Nora said, a catch in her voice.

"Adorable." Her mother rose to her feet again and sighed. "Your dad would have—" Dina's chin quivered and she turned away.

"Dad would probably have hidden them," Nora said bitterly. Mia had told her enough to be clear that Cliff had known about her existence, even if they'd never met. "He hid his daughter, why should his granddaughters be any different?"

That secrecy—the whole other family—stabbed at a tender place in Nora's heart. How was it possible for a man to have secrets that large and never let on? Didn't he feel guilty about it? Didn't something inside him jab just a little bit when he sat in church on Sunday? He had a reputation in this town, and this didn't line up with the way people saw him. She hoped that he did feel guilt—the kind to keep him up at night—because this wasn't just his private mistake; this had affected them all.

"Let's pick berries," her mother said.

But hidden or not, Nora's father would have fallen in love with these baby girls, too. He'd probably cherished a secret love for the daughter he'd never met. And hidden that love. So many lies by omission...

"Mom, if Dad had lived," Nora said, grabbing an ice cream pail and squatting at the start of a row, "what would you have done? I mean if Mia had suddenly dropped on our doorstep and announced herself, what then?"

"I'd have divorced him." There was steel in Dina's voice, and she grabbed a pail and crouched down next to Nora. They spread the leaves apart and began picking plump, red berries. "I had no idea he had someone else..."

"Mia said he wasn't in her life at all, though," Nora said. "Maybe the affair wasn't long-term."

Her mother shook her head. "I don't care how long it was. When your husband sleeps with someone else, there is nothing casual about it. It's no accident, either.

He chose to do the one thing that would tear my heart in two. He chose it."

"Do you hate him now?"

Her mother's voice was quiet. "I do this morning."

The berries were plentiful, and they picked in silence for a few minutes. Nora's mind was moving over her plans. If she kept these babies, she'd need help. She'd taken her twelve weeks of parental leave from her bookkeeping job, but when she went back to work again, she'd be paying for three children in day care. She couldn't afford that…not on her middling salary, and certainly not as a single mom. Staying in Hope to raise the girls would be the smart choice, but she hadn't taken her mother's emotional state into the equation. She didn't have her mother's support in keeping the babies, and she didn't have that little homestead where she could have set up house. She didn't have a job here, either, besides the family ranch. So she'd come home, unsure what the next step should be, but certain that this was the place where she could make her decisions.

They were halfway down the second row, six buckets filled with ripe, plump berries, when a neighbor's truck pulled into the drive.

"It's Jennifer," Dina said, glancing up. Then she added with a dry tone, "Great."

The neighbor woman hopped out of her truck and waved, then headed across the lawn toward them. She wore a pair of jeans and a loose tank top, a pair of gardening gloves shoved into her back pocket. She was also Dina's second cousin twice removed or something to that effect.

"Morning!" Jennifer called. She was in her early fifties, and her hair was iron gray, pulled back with a couple of barrettes.

"Morning." Dina looked less enthusiastic, but she met Jennifer's gaze evenly. "What brings you by?"

"Curiosity." Jennifer peered behind them at the stroller. "I heard about the triplets."

Nora watched as her mother pushed herself to her feet. It was already out there—their deepest pain being bandied about by the local gossips.

"Well…" Dina seemed at a loss for words.

"They're sleeping right now," Nora said, and she led Jennifer toward the stroller.

The older woman looked down at them then glanced at Dina.

"I had no idea Cliff was that kind of man. To live with a man for what—thirty-five years?—and you'd think you knew him."

"You'd think," Dina replied drily.

"So what happened?" Jennifer asked, plucking a berry from one of the filled buckets and tugging off the stem. "Did you see the signs?" She popped the strawberry into her mouth.

"Of my husband fathering another child?" Dina asked, anger sparking under the sadness. "What would that look like exactly, Jen?"

Jennifer's ex-husband was a known philanderer, while Nora's parents had always appeared to be the most devoted couple. Nora had never seen her parents fight—not once. Her father was a tough, unbending man, but somehow he and Dina could look at each other and come to a decision without saying a word. People commented on the strength of that marriage. Jennifer and Paul, however—everyone knew what Paul did on the side. And Jennifer and Paul had very public arguments about it on a regular basis.

"Paul was obvious," Jennifer retorted. "Cliff wasn't. I can normally point out a cheating man a mile away— I mean, I'm kind enough not to tell the wife, but I can spot it. Cliff didn't seem like the type."

Jennifer was enjoying this—there was a glimmer of gaiety under the external show of concern, the cheeriness of not being the one in the crosshairs for a change. But this was Nora's father being torn apart...and Nora couldn't help feeling a strange combination of anger at her dad and protectiveness toward him at the same time. He deserved to be raked across the coals—by Dina and Nora, not the town. He was *theirs* to resent, to hate, to love, to be furious with. The town of Hope, for all its good intentions, could bloody well back off.

"I don't want to talk about it," Dina replied shortly.

"Oh, I get it, I get it..." Jennifer hunched down next to a row of strawberry plants and beckoned toward the pile of empty buckets. "Pass me one, would you? I'll give you a hand."

They wouldn't get rid of her easily, it seemed, and Nora exchanged a look with her mother. This wasn't just her mother's shame, it was Nora's, too. Cliff had left them in this strange position of being pitied, watched, gossiped over. And in spite of it all, he was still her dad. Besides, she couldn't help but feel a little bit responsible for bringing this gossip down onto her mother's head, because she'd been the one to bring the babies here. Without the babies, no one would have been the wiser.

"It's scary," Jennifer prattled on, accepting a bucket and starting to pick. "I mean, will it affect the will? Do you remember the exact wording? Because if the wording is about 'children' in general, it includes any children he's had outside of wedlock, too. But if he names Nora specifically…"

There wasn't much choice but to keep picking, and Nora realized with a rush that keeping these babies in the family wouldn't be as simple as winning her mother over. Dina wasn't the only one who would be thinking about Cliff's infidelity when she looked at those girls—the entire town would.

Those babies represented a man's fall from grace, a besmirched reputation and hearts mangled in collateral damage. It wasn't that this town was cruel, it was that a sordid scandal was interesting, and people couldn't help but enjoy it a little. Gossip fueled Hope, Montana, and these three innocent babies had just brought enough fuel to last for years.

"You know what, Jennifer?" Nora rose to her feet and wiped the dirt off her knees. "I think Mom and I have it from here. Thanks, though."

The older woman looked startled then mildly embarrassed.

"Oh…yes, of course."

Jennifer wiped her own knees off and took some long steps over the rows of strawberry plants until she was on the grass again. They had an awkward goodbye, and then Jennifer headed back toward her vehicle. The gossip would be less congenial now, but it would have spiraled down into something nastier sooner or later anyway.

"Let's go eat some strawberries, Mom," Nora said, turning toward her mother. "And I want to sit with you on the step and dip our strawberries in whipped cream. Like we used to."

She wanted that whipped cream so badly that she ached. She wanted to rewind those angst-filled teenage years and bring back the sunny, breezy days where she'd been oblivious to heartbreak—when both of them had been. She wanted her mom—that calming influence, the woman who always had an answer for everything, even if that answer was "Some things we don't need to know."

"Okay." Dina nodded, and tears came to her eyes.

Everything had changed on them, spun and tipped. But they could drag some of it back, like whipped cream and strawberries on a warm August day.

THAT AFTERNOON EASTON came back to the house, his body aching from a day of hard work. He'd ridden Scarlet over to the southwest pasture to check up on the fence that was being rebuilt. Scarlet was his favorite horse; he'd bought her from the Mason ranch five years ago, and he and that horse had a bond stronger than most people shared. Scarlet was a good listener—recently, Easton had started talking. Not to people, but letting the thoughts form words and then spill out of him was cathartic. He could see why Nora had relied on him to just listen for all those years.

Out at the southwest corner, one of the ranch hands had broken a finger, so Easton sent him back, called the medic and took his place for the afternoon with the pole driver. He'd have to fill out a pile of paperwork for the injury, but the fence was complete and all in all it had been a good day.

Now, as he ambled up the drive toward the house, he was ready for a quiet evening. But he had to admit, he'd been thinking of Nora all day. He'd gotten used to her hurried trips back to the ranch, that wave across the yard. He'd made his peace with the fact that their friendship was something from long ago when she needed someone to listen to her problems. It had never been a terribly reciprocal friendship. He'd been quiet by nature, and she'd never asked too many questions. Maybe she'd assumed all was fine in his world because he didn't feel the need to vent.

As he came closer to the house he could hear the chorus of baby wails. Wow—it sounded like all three of them were crying. He picked up his pace, concerned that something might be wrong, and when he emerged from the mudroom, he was met by Nora's frantic face.

She stood in the middle of the kitchen—two babies crying from their little reclined bouncy chairs on the floor, and Bobbie in Nora's arms, also wailing.

"Everything okay?" Easton asked, dropping his hat onto a hook.

"No!" Nora looked ready to cry herself. "They've been like this for an hour…more? What time is it?"

"Almost five," he said.

"I'm so tired…" She patted Bobbie's diapered bottom and looked helplessly at the other two.

He couldn't very well leave them like that, and seeing those little squished faces all wet with tears, tiny tongues quivering with the intensity of their sobs, made him want to do something. He didn't know how to soothe an infant, but he could pick one up. He bent and scooped up the baby closest—Riley, he thought. But he could be wrong. He tipped her forward onto his chest and patted her back.

"Hey, there…" he murmured, looking down at her. She didn't look any happier, and he followed Nora's example and bounced himself up and down a couple of times to see if that improved the situation.

Nada.

He hadn't meant to start singing, but a tune came into his head in the same rhythm of his movement— a song he hadn't heard in a long, long time. Brahms's "Lullaby." He hummed it at first, and Riley stopped her hiccoughy sobs and listened, so he started to sing softly.

"Lullaby and good-night, hush my darling is sleeping.

On his sheets, white as cream, and his head full of dreams.

Lullaby and good-night…"

The baby lay her face against his chest and heaved in some shaky breaths. It was working—she liked the song…

He looked up to see Nora staring at him, an odd look on her face. She looked almost soothed, herself.

"I have an idea," she said, pointing to the couch in the living room. "Go sit there."

He did as she asked and sank into the couch. She deposited Bobbie next to her sister on his chest, and Bobbie had a similar reaction as Riley had, calming, blinking, listening as he sang. It was unexpectedly comfortable—the weight off his feet, two babies on his chest. Rosie still wailed from the kitchen, but when Nora scooped her up, she calmed down a little, and when Nora sank onto the cushion next to him, Rosie seemed to be lulled into quiet, too.

He sang the only verse he knew of that song a few times and the babies' eyes drooped heavier and heavier until they fell asleep, exhausted from their crying.

"I didn't know you could sing," Nora said softly.

"You never asked." He shot her a smile. "You know that cowboys sing. It soothes the herd."

"But they don't all sing well," she countered.

He chuckled softly. "I break it out when absolutely necessary."

There was an awful lot she didn't know about him. He knew more about her—she'd opened up with him. He knew that she hated sappy songs but loved sappy books, that her first horse had been her best friend and that her dad had been her hero. She'd talked and talked... But as he sat here with her, the babies breathing in a gentle rhythm, he wished he'd said more back then. She'd taken more than she'd given, but that hadn't been her fault. He'd given and given, and never asked for anything in return. Ever. Maybe he should have asked.

"I heard that song on TV years ago," he said. "I was maybe ten or eleven. I thought it was so beautiful that I nearly cried. So I tried to remember the words to it but could only remember the one verse. I imagined that one day my mother would come back and sing that song to me."

"Did you ever hear from her?" Nora asked quietly.

He shook his head. "Nope."

His mother left when he was eight, and he didn't have a solid memory of her. He knew what she looked like from the pictures, a woman with curly hair and glasses, one crooked tooth in the front that made her smile look impish. Those photos replaced his memories of her somehow—maybe because he'd spent more time with the pictures than the woman herself. His father had destroyed the other photos. "She left us," he used to say. "Don't even bother trying to remember her. She sure isn't thinking about us."

Easton couldn't trust his memories of her. He'd made up so many stories about her, so many situations that had never really happened, that he almost believed them. In his imagination, she was gentle and soft, and she stroked his hair away from his face. In his imagination, she loved him so devoutly that she'd never leave. When he lay in his bed at night, his dad drinking in front of the TV, he used to close his eyes and pretend that his mother was sitting on the edge of his bed, asking about his day. He'd imagined that well into his teen years…longer than he should have needed it.

"Do you know why she left?" Nora asked.

"She and Dad both drank a lot. They fought pretty

viciously. I don't know. She left a note that just said that she'd had enough. She was leaving, and we shouldn't try to find her."

"But she didn't take you with her," Nora pointed out.

Easton had questioned that over the years. If life was such hell here in Hope, why wouldn't she take her little boy along? Why would she leave him like that? She'd walked out, and he'd been left with an alcoholic father who could barely function. It was selfish. If she hadn't loved Dad, he could understand that. But why hadn't she loved *him*?

"Yeah..." He didn't have anything else to say to that. It was a fact—she'd left him behind.

"Do you remember her?" she asked.

"Not much," he admitted. "My dad dumped her stuff out into a pile and burned it. I guess that was cathartic for him. I managed to sneak off with one of her shirts—some discarded thing she didn't feel like bringing with her, I guess. I kept it under my mattress. It smelled like her cigarettes. I have that still."

"Why didn't I know about this?" Nora murmured.

A better question was, why had he told her now? Nora came from a loving home with parents who both adored her. Her family ran the ranch very successfully, and she'd had a bright future. He'd had none of those things, and yet he was still willing to be there for her, give her whatever support she needed. Why? Because he'd been in love with her, and maybe deep down he was afraid that if she knew the mess inside him, it would turn her off him.

"That's not how we worked, you and I," he said after a moment.

"Meaning I was self-involved." She winced. "I'm sorry. I must have been."

He shook his head. "I don't know. You were used to happier days than I was. You were more easily disappointed."

"I wish I'd been a better friend," she said.

But it wasn't friendship that would have soothed his teenage soul. If she'd been a more attentive friend, it might have made it harder. He might have actually held out hope that she'd see more in him. But being six inches shorter with a face full of acne had taken care of that.

"It's okay," he said. "It was a long time ago."

Easton needed to be careful, though, because not much had changed. She was still the heir to the ranch he worked, she was still the much loved daughter of the owner and she still needed his emotional support right now...except he wasn't so naive this time around. He knew how this ended. Nora would pull things together and she'd step out into that bright future of hers, leaving him right where he'd always been—on the ranch. She'd walk away again, and she wouldn't think to look back.

"You have the magic touch with the babies," she said, easing herself forward to stand up. "Thank you."

"No problem." What else was he supposed to do when three tiny girls had taken over his home? She walked toward the stairs with Bobbie in her arms.

"Why didn't you call your mom when the babies wouldn't stop crying?" he asked, and she looked back.

"Because she isn't really on board with this. Getting my mom's help isn't as great a solution as I thought. If I'm going to raise these girls, I'll have to figure out a way to do it on my own."

He'd suspected as much. While she'd probably pitch in, it was a bit much to expect Dina to joyfully embrace raising her late husband's other family.

"I'll get them back up to the crib," she said. "I'll be back."

And she disappeared from the room. He wasn't a long-term solution, either. He never had been, not in her eyes, and he wasn't about to make the same mistake he'd made as a teen. He didn't cross oceans for someone who wouldn't jump a puddle for him. Not anymore.

Chapter Four

That night Nora had managed to feed the babies without waking Easton, and when she got up again for their 6 a.m. feeding, Easton was gone, leaving behind percolated coffee cooling on the stove while he did his chores. She'd gone back to bed—her theory had been right and exhaustion made sleep possible—and when she opened her eyes at eight and got dressed, she'd found another pot of coffee freshly percolated on the stove. He'd been back, it seemed. And he'd be back for this pot, too, but she took a cup of coffee anyway—she desperately needed the caffeine kick.

The house felt more familiar without Easton around, and she stood in the kitchen, soaking in the rays of sunlight that slanted through the kitchen window, warming her toes. She sipped the coffee from a mug that said Save a Cow, Eat a Vegetarian. That was a sample of Easton's humor, apparently. She let her gaze flow over the details of this kitchen that she'd always loved...like the curtains that she'd sewn as a kid with the flying bluebird–patterned fabric. She'd made them in home ec, and she'd been so proud of them, despite the wandering hemline and the fact that one side was shorter than the other.

He kept those.

It was strange, because Easton hadn't kept much else of the original decor—not that she could blame him. The furniture and kitchenware had all been cast-offs from the main house. Anything of value—senti-mental or otherwise—had been distributed amongst the extended family when Great-Granny passed away. Easton's furniture was all new, and the kitchen had gleaming pots and pans. The dishes in the cupboard were a simple set of four of each dish, but they had ob-viously been recently purchased except for a few well-worn mugs like the one she was using now. There had been some renovations, too—fresh paint, some added built-in benches in the mudroom. He'd taken pride in this place.

And yet the floor was the same—patches worn in the linoleum by the fridge and stove. Though freshly painted, the windowsills still had that worn dip in the centers from decades of elbows and scrubbing. Nora used to stand by those windows while her elderly great-grandmother baked in the sweltering kitchen. She used to scoot past the fridge, wondering if Granny would catch her if she snagged another creamsicle. This old place held so many childhood memories, so many fam-ily stories that started with "When Great-Granny and Great-Grandpa lived in the old house..."

It felt strangely right to come back to this place, or it would have if Easton didn't live here. If her father had just done the normal thing and left everything to his wife, then she would be settling in here on her own—her future much easier to handle because of this family touchstone. But it wasn't hers—it wasn't *theirs*. Instead she felt like an interloper. She still felt like she needed permission to open the fridge.

It was after eight in the morning now. She'd fed the babies and changed their diapers, and now she was antsy to get outside into the sunshine. She'd thought she wanted space and quiet, but the silence was getting heavy. Solitude wasn't going to cut it. She needed a plan for her future, how she'd take care of these girls by herself, and that didn't seem to be formulating on its own.

The day was hot, and Nora had dressed the triplets in matching yellow sundresses—clothes that Mia had lovingly purchased and set aside for her daughters. The babies squirmed a little as Nora transferred them into the stroller outside the door, but once in the stroller, they settled back into deep slumber, tiny legs curled up around their diapers. She brushed a wisp of chocolate-brown hair away from Bobbie's forehead, love welling up inside her. It was dangerous to be falling in love with these girls, but she was.

Nora shut the door behind her and pushed the stroller over the dusty path that led from the house to the dirt road. The morning was still cool, the sun bright and cheerful in a cloudless sky. Dew still clung to the grass in the shady patches of lawn that Easton seemed to keep mowed around the little house. Thatches of rosebushes grew unfettered beside the sagging fence that encircled it. She paused at one and fingered a lush, white bloom.

Her father had been wrong in giving this house away. More than wrong—cruel. And what he'd been thinking, she had no idea. Easton was treating the house well, but no amount of appreciation or hard work would make him family, and this house belonged with family.

Had Dad been angry that she'd created a life for herself in the city? Maybe there was unspoken resentment she'd never known about. Nora pushed the stroller on, bumping onto the dusty road. The ditch beside the road was filled with long grass and weeds, but beyond that ditch, and beyond the rusty barbed wire fence, green pasture rolled out. The old barn stood a hundred yards off, grass growing up around it. Every year it bowed a little lower, hunching closer to the ground that longed to swallow it up. Her father had never been able to bring himself to tear the structure down. Cliff was a practical man in every sense, but when it came to that old barn, he used to say, "Leave it. It makes a pretty picture."

And yet he'd given away the house. Blast it—why couldn't his sentimental streak have stretched long enough to keep the house in the family? If he'd willed it to a cousin, she'd still be upset, but at least the person living there would have a personal connection to the family history.

The road led around to the main barn—a large, modern building—and as she walked, her nerves seemed to untangle. There was something about the open country that soothed her right down to the soul. There had been countless times in the city when she'd considered coming back, but things were complicated here in Hope. She and her mother had always been at odds, and Nora loved having her own space. She'd never been able to spread her wings under her parents' roof, in the same tiny town that would always see her as a kid.

As she crested a low hill, she spotted Easton a stone's throw down the road. A rusted pickup truck was parked at the side of the road, and the cattle were nearby the fence, a steer trying to push through a sagging stretch to reach the lush weeds beyond. Easton shouted something at the steer and waved his arms.

He had toughened into a tall, muscular man over the years. How had she failed to notice? His shirt was rolled up to expose his forearms, and he moved with the ease of a man accustomed to physical labor. But under the muscular physique was the same old Easton she'd always known—an uncomfortable combination of hardened muscle and old friend. It almost made her feel shy watching him work, and she'd never felt that way around Easton before. She'd always been the one in control, the one with all the power. Somehow the years had tipped that balance.

Nora picked up her pace—that was a two-person job by the look of that steer, but she had the babies with her, too. There was no way she could leave him alone with this.

"Easton!" she called.

He turned and spotted her. He pushed his hat back on his head and gave her a wave, then returned his attention to the fence. If he could get the steer to back up, she could staple up the barbed wire and the problem would be solved. She put the brakes on the stroller, making sure it was well off the road, then jumped the ditch.

"Give me the staple gun," she said.

He passed it to her then took off his hat and swatted the steer with it. "Come on," he grunted. "Get going!"

The animal bawled out a moo of frustration and took a few steps in reverse. Nora grabbed the barbed wire, pulled it taut and stapled it in one deft movement. She could feel the tongs of the wire pressing into her hand, but she didn't have time to complain. Then she grabbed the next wire down, being more careful this time where she touched it, and stapled again.

"Done," she said, stepping back.

"Thanks." Easton took the staple gun back and shot her a grin. "You're handier than you look."

"Accounting is tougher than you'd think," she joked.

Easton bent down and eased through the space between the wires, emerging on her side of the fence. He was closer than she'd anticipated, close enough for her to smell his musky scent. Her breath caught in her throat as she looked up at him. He was tall and broad. While those eyes hadn't changed, the rest of him certainly had.

"Is it?" he asked teasingly. "All those numbers and cushy office chairs?"

"I fixed the fence," she shot back. "And I have the blood to prove it." She held up her palm where the scratch had started to bleed.

"You okay?" Was that sympathy she saw in his eyes?

"It's a scratch, Easton. I'll survive it. Give me a hand over, would you?"

He jumped the ditch first then took her hand as she jumped across. He followed and she bent over the stroller, checking on the babies, who were all still asleep.

"Let's see that hand," he said, and she straightened, holding it out.

His touch was gentle and warm. "You'll need some antiseptic on that."

Nora turned the stroller around. "Yeah, I'll take care of it. Where's the first-aid kit in the house?"

"Never mind," he said. "I'll come along. I'm ready for my coffee anyway."

"What about the truck?"

He shrugged. "Not going anywhere."

It was nice to have his company, and if she didn't look over at the new, taller, stronger Easton, it almost felt like old times. Except that it wasn't.

"I'm sorry about when we were teenagers," she said after a moment. "When I was only focused on my own issues, I mean. I feel bad about that."

"It's okay," he said. "It was a long time ago. We've both come a long way since then."

"Maybe not as long as you think," she said wryly. "I also had a cup of your coffee."

He glanced over at her, dark gaze drilling into her for a beat longer than was comfortable.

"Okay, that's it," he deadpanned. "That's where I

draw the line." He paused. "You did leave me at least one mug, right?"

"Of course." She grinned.

Rosie woke up and squirmed, letting out a little whimper. Bobbie slept on, but Riley pushed out one tiny fist.

"Good morning, sleepyheads," Nora said.

The warm, low sunshine, these tiny girls, the sweet scent of grass carrying on the breeze, this good-looking cowboy walking next to her—it felt impossibly perfect, and the contentedness that rose up inside her was bittersweet. Staying in the old house—raising the girls here as would have been the plan if it weren't for her father's surprise will—wasn't an option. And having it so close, but just past her fingertips, made her ache for everything she couldn't keep.

She wanted to raise these girls, but she had to be realistic. She was an accountant, after all, and she knew how to look at a bottom line. And raising these girls alone didn't look possible.

Thanks a lot, Dad, she thought bitterly.

BACK AT THE HOUSE, Easton rummaged up the first-aid kit from under the sink and pulled out some iodine and some bandages, tossing them onto the counter. His coffee sat on the stove, the smell warming the room. He'd get himself a mug in a minute.

He'd been impressed by her quick thinking out there with the steer at the fence. She'd been around the heavy work on the ranch, of course, but when the men were working, Cliff made sure she kept a more supervisory position—out of the way. She was family, not a hired hand, and there had always been a line there. After her time in Billings, and now with her focus on the babies, he hadn't expected her to be on her game when it came to ranch work.

"I can do it," she said, taking the bottle from him. She winced as the brown drops hit the torn skin.

Nora had always been that rare combination of vulnerable and stubbornly independent. She needed people, but she wouldn't stick around for long. She was like a wild deer, leaping to her feet and dashing off the moment she'd regained enough strength. But while she sat next to him, close enough to touch, opening up about her internal world, it was possible to forget that the leap for freedom was in her nature.

Easton peeled the backing off the bandage and put it over the scrape. She smiled her thanks, ran her fingers over the bandage then moved toward the fridge.

Coffee. That was what he needed—his practical routine. He liked his coffee lukewarm—an oddity, he knew. But he liked what he liked, and his way of doing things provided for it. It had started when he was a young teenager, working part-time and trying to keep up with his schoolwork. He hated the taste of coffee back then, but it buzzed him enough that he could get everything done. And if he put enough cream in coffee, it ended up lukewarm. He preferred more coffee to cream now, but the lukewarm part remained oddly comforting.

And having Nora here was oddly comforting, too, as much as he hated to admit it.

"I'll get breakfast," Nora said, taking a mesh basket of eggs from the fridge. She paused to look down at the babies in their little bouncy chairs then glanced at her watch. "They'll need their bottles in an hour."

"I've already eaten." He put down his coffee on the counter and reached up for the slow cooker from the top of the cupboards. "But I'll start dinner."

Dinner was going to consist of pulled pork on some crusty rolls. The beauty of a slow cooker meant that the cooking could happen while he was out working. Single men had to suss up their dinner somehow, and he'd had a lot of practice in fending for himself. He had a whole lot less practice in providing for a family, though, even if they weren't his. He could have steeled himself to Nora again, but the babies complicated things. Or that was what he told himself. It was impossible to look down at a baby and refuse to feel something, and once he let in one feeling, the rest all tumbled in after it.

"You have Great-Granny's iron skillet!" Nora exclaimed, and he glanced over his shoulder.

"Your dad said I could have it if I wanted, and those iron skillets can go forever if you care for them right."

She looked like she was trying to hold back something between tears and anger, and he cleared his throat. Was that wrong to keep the skillet? He felt like he'd messed up somehow.

"Look, if you want it, take it," he said. "I can buy another one in town easy enough. It just seemed like a waste not to use it, that's all."

"I do want it," she said quickly.

"It's yours."

"Thank you."

Nora pulled a loaf of bread out of the bread box. She moved comfortably in this space—like she owned the place. But that didn't offend him this morning; it made him imagine doing this every day for the foreseeable future…her footsteps in the house, the scent of her perfume wafting through the place, navigating around her in the kitchen come breakfast time.

"Is that why you kept the curtains?" she asked as she cracked eggs into a bowl.

He glanced toward the window and shrugged. "I kept them for memory's sake. You told me how you'd made them to fit that exact window, and I—"

How to explain… He hadn't been able to take them down. They'd been something made by Nora, and she'd meant something to him. So he'd kept the curtains as a part of his own history—a piece of her.

"I guess I just thought they belonged. You can take them, too, if you want."

"No, that's okay." She kept her head down as she whipped the eggs. "They belong there. I'm glad they made the cut, that's all."

She tossed some butter into the pan and it sizzled over the heat. It looked like she was having French toast.

Easton grabbed the pork roast from the fridge and deposited it into the crock pot. An upended bottle of barbecue sauce was as complicated as it got. They worked in silence for a few minutes, the sound of frying filling the kitchen in a comforting way. He hated how good this felt—a quiet domestic scene. He wished that having another person in his space were more irritating, because he didn't want to miss her when she was gone. It would be easier if he'd be relieved to see her go.

Cliff had suggested that he find "some nice girl" and get married, but "some nice girl" wasn't going to be enough to wash out his feelings for Nora. He suspected Cliff was trying to be helpful. He'd never told the older man how he felt about Nora, but Cliff wasn't stupid, and Easton wasn't that great of an actor. But it wasn't going to be quite as easy as hooking up with a "nice girl," nor would it be fair to the woman who ended up with him.

"My great-grandparents had seven kids in this house," Nora said, breaking the silence.

Easton glanced at the ceiling, toward the two bedrooms upstairs. There was another room that could have been used for a bedroom off the living room downstairs, though he used it for storage.

"That would have been cozy," he said wryly.

"Well, there was a bit of a gap between the eldest two and the youngest five. So by the time the youngest baby came along, the eldest were getting married and leaving home."

"And your dad—" Easton had never heard too many details from Cliff. This was family land, accumulated over generations—he knew that much. Cliff had never expanded upon the story, though.

"My grandfather was the eldest, so he inherited the farm, and in turn left it to his eldest son, my dad," she said.

"And you'll inherit it next," he concluded.

"Yes." She pulled some French toast out of the pan and began soaking the next batch of bread.

"So why did you leave?" he asked.

Nora shot him an irritated look. "Did my dad complain about that?"

"No, I'm just curious," he replied. "You're next in line to run this place, and you take off for the city and get a degree in accounting. It doesn't make sense."

She was quiet for a moment then heaved a sigh. "Accounting is important for ranching these days. You need to know where the money is going and where it's coming from. If you don't have a handle on the numbers, it doesn't much matter how good you are with the cattle."

"Except that you didn't come back."

"Because I didn't want to," she snapped.

Easton was silent. She was ticked off now, and he wasn't quite sure which button he'd pushed. She was the one with all this family pride.

She sighed, and her expression softened. "I'm not living for a funeral," she said after a moment. "I've seen cousins doing that—constantly planning for the day they inherit, but my parents had me young. My mom is fifty-two. What am I going to do, spend the next twenty or thirty years living at home, trying to wrest the reins away from her? I could work with Dad really well, but you know exactly how well my mom and I get along. I had a choice—stay close to home and keep my thumb in the pie, or put some distance between us and have a life of my own. I chose to make my own life. I could always come back when they needed me, but coming back before then—"

She didn't have to finish the thought—he knew about the tensions between Nora and Dina. Nora had only ever visited for a few days at a time, and he knew that her stay in Hope would wear thin sooner or later. There had been a reason why she'd stayed away, and these babies didn't change the underlying problem.

"You won't be here for long, will you?" he asked.

"Probably not," she admitted. "I only have twelve weeks parental leave and I'll have to go back to my life in the city sooner or later."

"Okay." He wished his voice sounded more casual than it did, but he could hear the tension in it. He cleared his throat.

"Easton, I'm a grown woman."

"I know." He was painfully aware of that fact. "I just wanted to know what to expect. Thanks for telling me."

It suddenly occurred to him: she'd probably been counting on this house for when she did come back to stay. That would explain why she was so upset—her dad gave away her safety net. He didn't know how she planned to make this work with the babies, with the ranch, with her mom…but the old homestead would have been a convenient answer. Except he now owned the solution to her complicated situation, and he couldn't help but feel mildly guilty about that.

"I don't have a whole lot of options here in Hope," she said.

Her self-pity was irritating, though. She had actually

expected to waltz back into a life here at the ranch—at *her* convenience, not anyone else's.

"Not a lot of options?" He shot her an incredulous look. "You're the sole heir of six hundred acres. You have a university degree. Seriously, Nora. You're spoiled. You have every privilege and you don't even see it."

She blinked. "Did you just call me spoiled?"

Yeah, he had. If he was a little better rested, he might have rethought that one, but it was the truth. She always had been—her dad had mollycoddled her from the start. Nothing was too good for his little girl.

"Figure out what you're going to do," Easton said. "And for the record, I'm not pushing you out. I'm just not feeling as sorry for you as you'd like."

This was the thing—life was hard for everyone, not just Nora. In fact, life was arguably harder for pretty much everyone else. He could appreciate the position she was in, but she wasn't as stuck as she seemed to think.

"I didn't ask for your pity," she snapped. "And I *will* figure it out, but I'm not in any position to make promises about how long I'll be here."

Well, Easton wasn't in a position to make promises, either, and he had his own complications to sort out, without the benefit of a massive inheritance to come or a university degree to bolster him up. Cliff had left him this house for a reason, but the older man wasn't much of a talker. He'd told him that having someone living in the place full-time, someone with a stake in it, would take a load off his shoulders. Easton had even been considering renting the place from his boss, and then Cliff had passed away.

If he'd been a renter, would it still have been this awkward? Easton needed a few answers of his own if he was going to be able to go on living here, making a life out of this once-in-a-lifetime gift. He needed to know why Cliff Carpenter had given him this small patch of land, and ease his nagging conscience.

Chapter Five

The days here on the ranch were bleeding into each other. Maybe it was the lack of sleep or the constant feedings and diapers, but Nora was getting to the point where she wasn't even sure what day it was anymore. She'd had to check the date on her cell phone to be sure—it had been a full week now since she'd arrived. She had a doctor's appointment for the babies that she couldn't miss. She wasn't used to the blur of motherhood. It was exhausting in a whole different way than she was used to—no breaks, no turning off. At least in her bookkeeping job she could leave the office and turn off her phone. She could have silence, a bubble bath, let her mind wander. But with the babies, she was on constant alert, listening for cries or thinking ahead to feedings...

The last few days, she and Easton had been on egg shells. He'd been out a lot, checking fences and cattle—more than was necessary, it seemed to her. And she'd been trying to stay as polite as possible, to keep her intrusion to a minimum. This wasn't going to last, and one of these days, she had a feeling one of them was going to snap again.

Today Nora could use another nap—the only way she seemed to get sleep these days—and she was about to try to lie down for ten minutes when her cell phone rang. She seriously considered ignoring it, but when she saw the name on her screen, she relented. It was Kaitlyn Mason, her oldest friend.

"Why didn't you let me know you were in town?" Kaitlyn asked when she picked up.

"It's complicated…" Nora confessed.

"Yeah, so I heard. Even more reason for a friend, right? You need coffee. I'm sure of it. And you need to vent."

"And you need to tell me about married life," Nora added. "I haven't seen you since the wedding. It's been like two years. Wow."

"See?" Nora could hear the smile in Kaitlyn's voice. "It's an absolute necessity. Now, do I come to you, or do we meet up in town?"

It would be nice to get out alone, if that was possible. Was it? Or was that selfish, like Easton has accused her of? Just then Riley started to whimper—very likely a wet diaper. She poked a finger into the top and felt dampness. Yep, wet diaper. Was it wrong to want some time to herself this badly? And was it normal to feel guilty about it?

"I'm going to call my mom and see if she can watch the babies," Nora said. "I'd love to get out to see you for a couple of hours—alone. I'll call you back, okay?"

So Nora changed Riley's diaper, and then Bobbie's and Rosie's, too. Then she dialed her mother. Dina agreed to look after the girls for a couple of hours, and

Nora felt a weight lift off her shoulders. Still, she felt that same nagging guilt—not only because she was getting some time off, but also because her mother was going to be looking after Mia's babies. Doing this alone was hard…really hard. And this was what grandmothers were for, right? Grandmas were on a whole different level than babysitters. If these weren't Mia's babies, but Nora's own, she wouldn't feel any guilt at all about having her mother babysit. Her own grandmother had watched her on a regular basis when she was young, and she'd treasured that relationship. Her grandma had played with her, told her stories and after a few hours together would look down into her face and say, "You are such a special girl, Nora." The triplets deserved to have a grandma who thought they were special girls, too.

When Nora arrived at the main house a few minutes later, her mother helped her to unload the babies from their car seats and get them settled inside. They were awake by then, and three pairs of brown eyes stared up solemnly from their bouncy chairs. Dina squatted next to the babies, her expression melancholy.

"They've all been fed and changed," Nora said. "Their next bottle is due at 2:30, but I find it helps to start about fifteen minutes early. I feed Rosie or Riley first and feed Bobbie last. She's able to wait a little more patiently than the other two. Riley can't stand a wet diaper, so if she cries, you can be pretty positive it's that. If you change Riley, it's a good idea to change the other two at the same time, otherwise it gets really overwhelming. Rosie is a snuggler, and she'd stay in your arms the whole time if you let her. I don't like Bobbie to be neglected, though, just because she's a little stronger—"

"Sweetheart." Dina stood up and put a hand on Nora's arm. "We'll be okay."

Would they? It wasn't really the babies she was worried about; it was her mother. This couldn't be an easy task for her. Dina regarded her with misty eyes. Suddenly, the strong, resilient woman who had strode through Nora's life with an answer for everything looked fragile.

"Mom, are you all right?"

Dina wiped an errant tear from her cheek.

"It's not what you think."

"Do they remind you—"

"No, no." Dina shook her head. "I mean, of course they do, but it's not that. It's just that I remember knowing you that well, once upon a time. You liked being on my hip every waking hour, and you'd toddle around in a wet diaper for hours. You hated being changed."

"I grew up," Nora said with a small smile. "It happens to the best of us."

"I know, but I could make anything better for you back then. I can't anymore." Dina sighed. "And while you grew up, I never stopped being your mom."

There had been a time when her mother had been able to predict every passing mood that Nora had, but that was in the days of strawberry-picking and whipped cream. If she raised these girls, would they drift away one day, too? Would she lose this ability to make things right for them?

Nora was tired, overwhelmed. She hadn't slept properly since the babies arrived almost two weeks ago, and every waking moment was taken up with diapers and bottles, crying and soothing…all times three.

"Mom, you doing this—taking care of the babies for a couple of hours—this is just what I need right now. And I really appreciate it."

And she meant that with every fiber of her being.

"Well." Dina cast her daughter a smile. "I'm glad."

Nora adjusted her purse on her shoulder and looked down at the babies. "I've been thinking about it lately… And I'm not sure that I'll be able to, but I want to keep these girls. And if I would be Mom to them, that will make you their grandmother…sort of. Right?"

Dina winced and swallowed hard. "I'm not their grandmother. Angela Hampton is their grandmother."

"Angela's dead," Nora replied. "And so is Mia."

"We're the *other* family." Dina's eyes glittered with tears. "It's not the same. I know you love them, sweetheart, but it's not the same at all."

If they were looking for *the same*, they could stop searching. Nothing would be the same again—Nora's father was gone, and his memory was tarnished. The security she'd had in her parents' marriage had been whipped out from under her. That was the thing—she was just recognizing it now: her father's affair had taken away her ability to trust. If she couldn't trust her own father, how could she trust anyone? Even an old friend like Easton suddenly became suspect.

"No, it's not the same as if I were the natural mother, but we're all the babies have," Nora countered.

"You're not the one who was cheated on," her mother replied. "It's easier for you. These girls are the grandchildren of the woman who slept with my husband behind my back. They belong to your idiot father and that woman—together. And I'm left out of that."

Did her mother think that Nora was unaffected by her father's infidelity? She'd been affected—very deeply—but she also had three innocent babies looking to her for love and comfort. She'd been thrown into the deep end of motherhood, and she didn't get the luxury of sifting through her feelings.

"This *isn't* easy for me," she retorted. "My dad cheated on my mom. That's not pretty. That's not pleasant. I had a half sister I never knew—a half sister I shouldn't have had. My role model for what to look for in a husband of my own turned out to be the wrong kind of man."

"I'm just suggesting that you think it through," her mother said, her tone tense. "Because I'm not Grandma. I can't be."

That felt like a rejection to Nora—of the babies, but also of her. "You actually could," Nora replied, emotion catching her throat. "If you chose to be. You're *my* mother."

"I can't…" Her mother shook her head, sorrow shining through her eyes.

Nora could see the truth in her mother's words. This wasn't about what should be or what could be…this was about what her mother could give and what she couldn't. She'd had her heart broken twice—first by her husband's death, and then by the revelation that he hadn't been faithful. Dina couldn't be the grand-mother Nora needed her to be. She couldn't look down into these girls' faces and tell them how special they were ...

"I'll cancel with Kaitlyn," Nora said.

"For crying out loud, Nora, I'm not a monster." Her mother tugged a hand through her hair in exasperation. "I can babysit."

Nora met her mother's misty gaze. Right now all Nora wanted was for her mother to become that strong, resilient font of all answers again. She wanted to hear her mother say that everything would be all right, and that they'd figure this out together. But that wasn't going to happen, because everything would not be all right. Everything was broken.

"Thanks, Mom," Nora said past the lump in her throat. "I won't be more than a couple of hours."

Nora shut the door and headed out to her truck. She'd come home because she couldn't imagine doing this alone, but it didn't look like she'd have much op-tion. If she kept these babies, she'd be a single mom in every way.

THAT AFTERNOON WHEN Easton came back to the house for a coffee, he found a note on the fridge from Nora saying that she'd gone out for a few hours. It was strange, because coming back to the empty house had been all he'd wanted lately—to get back to normal—but it felt lonely, too. He'd started getting used to having her around, was almost tempted to call out "I'm home!" when he got back from working in the fields.

When he'd gotten back to the house after their argument, they'd both apologized for being too harsh and agreed that being both overtired and under the same roof was stressful for the both of them. So he'd been trying to be a more gracious host. He wasn't sure if it was working or not, because Nora was almost too nice to him lately, too—like someone who didn't know him well enough to be straight with him. And they had enough history to make that flat-out wrong. Regardless, there had been no more fights.

That afternoon he'd ridden out to the north field to check on the bulls, and on the way, he'd talked to Scarlet about the whole situation. Except that talking to Scarlet only made him realize all the things he wanted to say to Nora—if they weren't in the middle of this politeness standoff, that is.

Cliff had advised him to find a nice girl, and maybe he should do that. This time with Nora could be used to get her out of his system, and then he should look around next time he was at church and start thinking more seriously about filling up this house with a family of his own. Playing house wasn't going to suffice.

Easton had an hour or so before he needed to head out to the barn and check up on a sick cow, and without Nora here, he had a chance to do something he'd put off for too long. He gulped back some coffee then headed up the narrow staircase to the top floor. He paused, looking up at the attic door in the ceiling above.

Easton had seen a couple of boxes in the attic when

he'd moved in. When he'd peeked inside, they looked like Cliff's things so he'd let them be. Maybe it was grief, or he'd simply been too tired to deal with the boxes then, but now that Nora had made him question why Cliff had left him the house, he'd been thinking about those boxes again. Maybe there'd be a few answers. And maybe not. Cliff had left these boxes in the homestead for a reason, and Easton suspected it was because he hadn't wanted his wife and daughter to know about them.

He pulled on the cord, and the attic stairs swung slowly down. He unfolded them and they hit the wooden floor with a solid thunk. He climbed the narrow steps and ducked as he emerged into the A-frame room above. A single bulb hung nearby, and he clicked it on.

The attic was dusty but otherwise clean. An old single-width metal bed frame leaned against one side, half-rusted. A couple of cardboard liquor boxes were stacked next to it, and beside them some rat traps which were, thankfully, empty. There wasn't much else up here—probably cleaned out when the original owners died. He loved the feel of the attic—the warped panes of glass in the two square windows at either end of the room, the knot holes in the floorboards and the sense of lives lived for decade upon decade in this old house.

Easton had to duck to keep from hitting his head on the slanted roof, and he pulled the first box toward him and squatted next to it. He opened the flaps and peered inside. He found a worn denim jacket, a pair of old cowboy boots, a chipped coffee mug—nothing that looked terribly precious. Underneath the boots was nestled an old manila envelope. He took it out.

The envelope hadn't been sealed. Inside were what appeared to be a few old letters and a handful of photos. Easton sorted through the photos first. One was of a newborn, all bundled up, the date September 12, 1988 written on the bottom next to Mia's full name: *Mia Alexandra Sophia Hampton.* Angela hadn't used the Carpenter name for their daughter. There were a few pictures of a blonde toddler with her brown-haired mother. Angela was rounded, with a full bust and ample hips. She was attractive enough, and Easton paused, looking at the photo, trying to imagine Cliff Carpenter with this woman. Angela wore a little too much makeup for Easton's taste, but he could see her love for the little girl in her arms, and that was what mattered. A few years of photos seemed to be missing, and then a school picture of Mia as a blonde little girl with braces and freckles, and then as a teenager without braces. Mia had been quite lovely. Next was a snapshot of her as a young woman in front of a Route 66 sign, squinting into the sunlight. She had her mother's full bust and ample hips, but her face looked more like the Carpenters. There was something in her sparkling blue eyes that reminded him of Nora.

Easton sighed, putting the photos aside. Mia had grown up, and Cliff had known about his daughter, apparently. He looked at the address on the envelopes—a PO box in town. Cliff had gone out of his way to keep this hidden. There were about a dozen letters, and he picked one at random.

These probably weren't his business. Cliff hadn't meant them to be anyone's business. Still, Easton would take a look and see what was here. If it was damning enough, he would burn the lot and let Cliff keep some posthumous privacy. But there was the chance that this might give Nora and her mother a few answers.

The first letter he opened was dated May, 1998.

Dear Cliff,

Mia is doing well. She's getting As and Bs in school, and the money you sent will go for her summer camp. Her best friend is going and she's been pleading to be allowed to go for months now, so your money couldn't have arrived at a better time. She still wants to play the violin, but I can't afford the lessons, or the instrument. I've looked into it, but it's just too much. Maybe you could consider helping her with that if her interest doesn't change.

Thank you for your support. You should know that she's been asking more and more questions about why she doesn't have a dad. The other kids have dads, even if they aren't in their lives. It would mean a lot to her to know your name, at least. She wouldn't have to contact you. I know you have your family and we wouldn't interfere. Please reconsider letting me tell her.

Angela.

The next letter was dated December, 2008.

Dear Cliff,
Thank you for the recent money. Mia is working
two jobs to pay for her college tuition, and she's
exhausted. She's switched majors, and now she's
taking Education. She wants to teach elemen-
tary school. The money you sent will help to buy
books next semester, and she's very grateful. She
asked me to thank you.

I have some bad news. I've had back pain for
a few months, and finally went to a doctor about
it. It's cancer—stage 3. It's in my spine—quite
treatable—and in my liver. There's hope, and
I'll fight it, but my insurance will only go so far.
I have no intention of dying yet—our daughter
still needs me. I haven't told Mia yet, though. She
needs to focus on her studies.

If the worst should happen, don't forget about
your daughter.
Angela.

It looked like Angela had told Mia about her father
at some point. Easton knew from Nora that Angela
had passed away, and he could only assume it was
from the cancer.

He opened another envelope, and this one was different than the others—written in a child's hand. His breath
caught in his throat as he scanned the printed words:

Dear Dad,
I only call you Dad because I don't know your
name, because if I knew your name, I'd call you

that. But Mom—Mom was underlined three times—*says she'll mail this to you, and I can say anything I want to you. So here goes.*

I hate you. I think you're awful. You don't even know me, and you don't want me. I'm a nice person. My friends say that I'm too good for a deadbeat dad like you. I don't care that you send money, because I don't want any of it. You can keep it and spend it on whatever stupid stuff you buy yourself.

My mom loves me and we do just fine on our own. We don't need you, and we don't need your money. So if you don't want to know me, and I'm a super-good person, you know, then you can get lost.

But if you wanted to know me, you'd find out that I'm pretty smart, and I'm nice to people, and I love animals, and my favorite color isn't purple like every girl in my class, it's green. And I'm going to be a marine biologist when I grow up. That's what you'd find out, and you'd probably like me, too. But you don't get to find out how nice I am, because even if you wanted to meet me, I'd say, "Sorry, I'm too busy being super-nice and super-fun."

Without any love at all,
Mia Hampton.

There was a PS tagged at the end in Angela's handwriting: *I'm sorry about Mia. She's really angry right now, but I promised I'd send this letter no matter what.*

We do need the money. One day she'll understand how much you provided. I promise you that.—A

The poor kid. Her loneliness, her anger, her desperation to be wanted by her dad—it all just shone through that letter, and Easton couldn't help but wonder how Cliff had dealt with all of that. Obviously, he had never told his wife and daughter about the other little girl out there who hated him because she wanted to be loved so badly.

Had Cliff ever written his daughter back? Or had that letter gone unanswered? Easton wished he knew, but everyone concerned had passed away.

Nothing else was in the box, and the one underneath it held only an incomplete set of old encyclopedias.

This child hadn't been a secret from Cliff, obviously, but it also didn't look like the affair was long-lived. Angela had never seemed to be pleading for anything, and Easton wondered if that would be a relief to Nora on some level. Maybe it was a one-time mistake and not some lifetime of philandering.

This was an odd relief to Easton, he had to admit. He'd always looked up to Cliff, and his fall from grace had hit Easton, too. He knew what it was like to have a disappointing father. He'd grown up with a father who embarrassed him constantly and hadn't been able to provide for him. But Cliff had been different—principled, successful, solid. Cliff had been the kind of man Easton would have wanted in a father, and he'd become a sort of father figure to him over the years. So finding out that Cliff had another child out there—

that had hurt his sense of decency, even if Easton didn't have a right to feel it.

"You weren't my dad," he muttered.

But even with this mess, Nora was lucky. She still had more than she thought she did because while her father had been flawed, Cliff had at least been there for her. He'd raised her, provided for her, taught her what he could. Easton probably had more in common with Mia—standing on the outside of something they'd never have. So while Cliff's fall from grace was disappointing, it wasn't a betrayal to Easton. At least it wasn't supposed to be.

It hung heavy around his neck, but mostly he felt sorry for Cliff… In life, the man had been respected, admired, trusted. If Cliff had lived to see this, he'd have been crushed.

Maybe it was too late to offer, but this was one thing Easton could give his late boss: absolution, from him, at least. Because Cliff owed him nothing.

Chapter Six

Nora arrived at The Vanilla Bean coffee shop and parked in the angled parking out front. She could feel the pressure leaking out of her. She needed a break, and she still wasn't sure if that made her a bad mother. All she knew was that she felt lighter already for having driven by herself without three infants in the back of her truck.

"Kaitlyn!" Nora wrapped her arms around her friend and gave her a squeeze. "It's so good to see you!"

The Vanilla Bean hadn't changed a bit over the years. It still sported the same framed photos from decades past—Main Street before the murals had been painted, the old grain elevator in use, a grinning bull rider having won a ribbon in the 1957 county fair. There was also a bookshelf with a sign above that read "Lending Library—take a book, leave a book." Nora had read her first romance novel from that shelf—a scandalous secret that she hid from her parents and read out by the barn. This place held the town's history as well as their own, and no matter how long she stayed away, there was a part of her that counted on places like the Vanilla Bean to stay exactly the same.

Kaitlyn had put on a little weight since Nora had seen her last, but it suited her—adding some roundness to her figure. And she wore her hair in a bob now. Kaitlyn's eyes crinkled as she smiled. She motioned toward the table by the window where two coffees were already waiting. "I hope you aren't dieting, because I got you a mochaccino—for old time's sake."

They felt oh so grown up when they'd come here as teens. The last time they'd been here was just before Kaitlyn's Christmas wedding a couple of years earlier. Nora slid into the seat and pried the lid off the cup. This felt good to be out, away from it all for a little while. She watched as two pickup trucks going in opposite directions down the street stopped so that the drivers could talk through open windows.

"It's perfect," Nora said. "So how are you?"

"I'm good." She sipped her drink and licked her lips. "I'm not pregnant—that's what everyone asks. I swear, you gain a pound and everyone wants to be the first one to call it."

"They don't." Nora grimaced.

"They do." Kaitlyn nodded. "But it's okay. I survive it. Everyone is doing it to Nina, too, so I feel better."

"How is Nina?" Nora asked. Kaitlyn's sister had a bit of a scandalous past, having cheated on her fiancée who was fighting in Afghanistan and marrying his best friend while he was away.

"Their son is two now—smart as a whip, that kid. He already knows his alphabet. She's exhausted, but happy…but exhausted. So Brody and I wanted some time alone before we threw ourselves into that."

"I don't blame you," Nora agreed. Kaitlyn's husband came back to Hope when he was wounded in the war, and he was still recovering emotionally. "I'm exhausted, too, and it's only been a few days with the babies. It's harder than I thought."

"So what's going on?" Kaitlyn asked. "I heard a few rumors, but…"

Nora gave as brief an explanation as possible, and as the words came out, she felt relief. She'd been taking this one step at a time from discovering her half sister's existence to becoming the mother of three newborns overnight, and Kaitlyn's expression of sympathy and disbelief was comforting. Her life had turned upside down in a matter of weeks, and some sympathy helped.

"How are you and your mom dealing with all this?" Kaitlyn asked.

"We're—" Nora paused. Were they even dealing with it? They were stumbling through it, not exactly handling anything besides putting one foot in front of the other. "We're in shock still, I think," she concluded. "Thank God Mackenzie thought of us and sent a triplet stroller. I didn't even know where to start."

"Mackenzie is great," Kaitlyn agreed.

"The funny thing is, I keep seeing married couples having babies everywhere I go," Nora confessed. "Mack and Chet have three now, right? And here I am with three babies and no husband…or boyfriend. And the explanation is just so freaking complicated."

"Look, you'll feel like you have to explain yourself

no matter what. I'm married, and everyone is anxious for me to have a baby. If you're not married, everyone is anxious to find you someone. There's no point in worrying about public opinion, because you'll always be lacking in something. Those babies are lucky to have you."

"Are they?" Nora sighed. "The truth is, I can't afford them. Not alone. That's why I came home. I was hoping that I could sort something out with my mom so we could take care of them together. I could quit my job in the city and come back to Hope and find something part time in bookkeeping and put the rest of my time into the girls. But that's not really an option."

"And there's no help?" Kaitlyn asked.

"I'm a bookkeeper, Kate." Nora shook her head. "I work hard. I have a one-bedroom apartment in Billings. I can't afford day care, a bigger place in a decent part of town, clothes, formula, diapers... It's overwhelming. And if I can't sort something out—"

She didn't want to finish the thought out loud, because she hadn't actually admitted it to herself until now. She'd have to give the babies up to another family that could give them the life she couldn't provide herself.

The thought caught her heart in a stranglehold, and for a moment, she felt like she couldn't inhale. Give them up. That was the obvious solution that she'd been avoiding looking at all this time. She'd been hoping that something would present itself—some solution that would make it all come together.

"*Would* you give them up?" Kaitlyn asked quietly.

Nora shook her head. "I really don't want to, but I have to wonder what's best for them. My mom can't be a grandmother to them…they remind her of what my dad did to her. How do you explain that to your kids—this is my mother, but don't call her Grandma. It's not right. The girls would be the ones to suffer."

"I can understand that, though," Kaitlyn said. "If I found out that Brody had cheated on me—even that many years ago—and I was supposed to just accept his child by another woman, or his grandchild… That's a lot to ask."

"I know." It all felt so impossible. "I don't know what to do. Eventually, I'll have to figure something out."

"Maybe give it time?" Kaitlyn suggested.

Did time make it better or worse? That depended on whether her mom changed her mind about this. If she didn't, then Nora would have taken even more time to fall in love with the babies before she had to let them go.

"I'm not sure," she confessed. "But that's okay. I was hoping to hear all the news today, not wallow in my own self-pity. How are Dakota and Andy?"

Dakota had married Andy Granger just before Kaitlyn and Brody got married. Andy sold his half of the ranch he and his brother inherited and then left town. Everyone hated him at that point, because he'd sold out to some big city yahoos. But then he came back to help run a cattle drive for his brother, and Dakota had been hired onto the team. She'd hated him, but something happened on that drive that changed it all, because when they got back, they got engaged.

Tears misted Kaitlyn's eyes, and Nora felt a flash of alarm. What had she said? She reached out and took her hand. Kaitlyn swallowed a couple of times and blinked back tears. Something was wrong. Here she'd been so focused on her own life that she'd completely missed that something was deeply wrong in her friend's.

"What's going on, Kate?" Nora asked, leaning forward.

"Dakota's pregnant. Andy is over the moon—you've never seen a happier guy. He keeps trying to do things for her, and Dakota is all hormonal and wants to kill him." Kaitlyn forced a smile, although it didn't reach her eyes. "It's cute. If he survives this pregnancy, they'll make great parents."

"And yet you're crying," Nora said. Those hadn't been sympathetically happy tears.

Kaitlyn was silent for a moment, then she licked her lips. "I can't seem to get pregnant. Everyone else around me is either pregnant or a new mom… You aren't the only one noticing it. We've been trying since the honeymoon. I told you that we're just taking some time to be a couple, but that's not even true."

"Oh, Kate…"

"I was never the baby fever type. I just assumed that since we were…doing all the things it takes to make a baby…that it would just happen. Like with Nina. Like with Dakota. Like with every woman I seem to come across! This is supposed to be natural."

"It'll happen…" Nora said, but she knew she couldn't

promise that any more than Kaitlyn could assure her that she'd find the man of her dreams. Sometimes life didn't pan out the way you wanted it to. Sometimes deeply devoted couples remained childless. Sometimes good women didn't find their guy.

"It'll happen when it happens," Kaitlyn agreed. "We're doing all the right things—on a daily basis." A smile flickered across her face. "I shouldn't complain, should I?"

Nora laughed softly. Considering that Kaitlyn had a gorgeous husband to "do all the right things" with on a *daily* basis... She felt some heat in her cheeks. "They say the trying is the fun part, don't they?"

"They do say that." Kaitlyn smiled and wiped her eyes. "Sorry, I honestly didn't want to talk about this. I was supposed to be *your* supportive friend. So where are you staying? With your mom?"

"No, in the old farmhouse," Nora said. "With Easton, actually."

Kaitlyn's eyebrows rose, and she paused in the wiping of her eyes. "With Easton? How is that?"

"You know my father left him the homestead in his will, right?"

"I'd heard." Kaitlyn winced. "I'm sorry about that."

"Well, he has a guest bedroom so I'm using that with the babies. My mom can't deal with three newborns right now, and it's all so complicated, so this is a way to give her some breathing space. There isn't a huge amount of room in the homestead, but we're squeezing in."

"I'm not asking about sleeping arrangements," Kaitlyn replied with a quirky smile. "Unless I should be?"

"No!" Nora leaned back in her chair. "I haven't changed that much."

"But how is it with Easton?" Kaitlyn pressed. "I remember how crazy he was about you."

That was an exaggeration. Kaitlyn had always thought that Easton was in love with her, but Nora never believed it. They were friends, that was all. They talked about her boyfriends and sometimes went riding together. Easton had a bit of a crush for a while, but they'd moved past that.

"It wasn't as exciting as you think," Nora replied.

"You're wrong there." Her friend finished wiping her eyes. "What he felt for you was significantly more than friendship."

Had Easton really felt more for Nora? She'd thought that Easton got a lot from their friendship…like friendship. But maybe she'd been the naive one.

"I didn't think it was anything more than me hitting puberty first," she admitted.

"Do you remember that one birthday—I think you turned fifteen—when the girls snubbed you, and I was the only one to show up at your party?" Kaitlyn asked. "I think Easton had just started working at your place, and he brought you those wildflowers from the far pasture."

"That was sweet," Nora agreed. Easton had always been thoughtful that way, and she'd often thought that whatever girl he settled down with would be lucky to have him. He'd be a good boyfriend—to someone else.

She just hadn't been attracted to him. And it wasn't because of his acne—that wasn't his fault, and she wasn't that shallow. He was a good friend, but she couldn't make the leap to something more.

"And when you broke up with whatever guy you were dating, who was there to talk you through it?"

"I get it, I get it." Nora shrugged weakly. "He was a decent guy—more than decent. I just wasn't interested back then."

"And now?" Kaitlyn asked.

"Now?" Nora shook head. "*He* isn't interested anymore, either. That's all in the past."

"Oh. That's too bad, because he most certainly grew up." She shot Nora a meaningful look.

Nora wasn't oblivious to how ruggedly good-looking Easton had turned out to be, but she chuckled. "He's not the same guy willing to do anything to make me happy anymore. So you can rest easy on that. He's willing to tell me what he really thinks of me now, and frankly… it's better this way."

Spoiled. That had been his descriptor. She'd been rather shocked to have Easton talk to her like that, but it was better than leading him on. The last thing she needed was to be pussyfooting around Easton's feelings. She had enough to worry about with the babies, with her mom…

"That *would* be better," Kaitlyn agreed. "For him, at least."

"Besides," Nora said. "He came out on top. He's walked away with three acres and my family's history."

"Did he know your father was changing his will?"

Kaitlyn took a sip of her latte. "He was getting a lot of job offers at bigger ranches. He's good, you know. Your dad must have kept him around by putting him into the will."

That would actually make sense. Maybe her father hadn't signed it over because of tender feelings—it was possible he'd been negotiating with his ranch manager. That would make everything different...including her view of Easton. Her father had kept secrets—why not one more? Could it really come down to something as common as holding on to a skilled employee?

If that were the case, then Easton would be a whole lot less innocent than he appeared. Could he have actually been angling for that land? He'd said he wasn't, but he wouldn't be the first man to lie to her, either.

"You might be onto something," Nora said. "I've been going over this in my head repeatedly, trying to figure out why my dad would do that... It's like I never knew him."

"You know as well as I do that a good ranch manager is worth his weight in gold," Kaitlyn replied. "Easton is honest. He works like a horse. He's smart, too. My dad has said more than once that if he could afford Easton, he'd try to lure him over to our ranch."

"He wouldn't." Nora frowned.

"My dad?" Kaitlyn shrugged. "Maybe."

Mr. Harp was a jovial guy—but he was also a shrewd rancher. There was a strange balance with the Hope ranches—they were neighbors who supported each other and helped each other out, but they were also in competition for the best employees. The ranch would one day be hers, and it affected the way she'd looked at their land—including the three acres her father had left to Easton.

Easton could take another job if he wanted to. But another possibility made her stomach sink: maybe Easton was less of a nice guy than she'd always assumed. Just because he'd had a rough childhood didn't make him some kind of saint. Easton had some negotiation room, and he may have taken advantage of that.

"Who was trying to get Easton?" she asked.

"Not us," Kaitlyn said with a shake of her head. "But rumor around town was that some larger ranches out of state were putting their feelers out for experienced managers. A lot of people were mad. It's not nice to poach someone's manager after they've spent years grooming him."

Nora had no idea. Was it possible that she'd been duped by more than just her father?

EASTON SAT IN the easy chair in the living room, listening to the sounds of Nora putting the babies to bed. Her voice was soft, the gentle tones carrying through the floorboards, but the words were muffled. It didn't matter what she was saying, of course. It was the comforting lilt that the babies would respond to.

His mom had never been that way—not that he could remember, and certainly not according to the stories his father had told him.

The stairs creaked as Nora made her way down and Easton looked away. He liked having her here, but he was getting increasingly aware of her presence. She was his guest and in his home, yet he still felt like he shouldn't be listening to the soft rustle of her moving around his home—like that was overstepping somehow. He certainly shouldn't be enjoying it.

"They're almost asleep," Nora said, emerging into the living room. She tapped her watch. "Three hours and counting."

She'd been distant all evening—polite, but closed off.

"You tired?" he asked.

"Always." She smiled wryly.

He'd been debating how much he should tell Nora, if anything, all afternoon. Was it his place? What would Cliff have wanted? And how could he possibly know? He shouldn't be in the middle of all this family drama—but maybe he should have seen complications coming.

"I went through the attic today," he said.

Nora sank into the recliner kitty corner to the couch and stifled a yawn. "Was there anything up there?"

He couldn't shoulder Cliff's secrets alone. He wasn't even sure it was fair of him to keep the letters to himself. Cliff wasn't his father, and Nora was the one who would live with a lifetime of questions.

"Your dad had put a box of personal effects up there," Easton said. "I saw it when I moved in but then forgot about it. I remembered it today, and I thought I'd take a look through it."

"My dad did?" She shot him a sharp look. "Why would he do that?"

Easton pushed himself to his feet and retrieved the

box from the other side of the sofa. The contents would answer her questions better than he could.

"I don't know, exactly," he said. "But he did."

"That isn't true, though, is it?" She put a hand on top of the box but didn't look at it. Her gaze was fixed icily on him.

"What do you want from me?" he demanded. "Nora, this is awkward. I'm not supposed to be in the middle of your family issues. I found a box with your dad's things in it, and I'm handing it over."

"I had coffee with Kaitlyn Mason today."

That was supposed to mean something to him? Kaitlyn and Nora had been friends since school days. "Great. Glad you got out."

He was frustrated. He was a private man who had been sharing his personal space for a week now with a woman he used to love, and having her here with him, sleeping in the next room and sharing his living space... He was liable to start feeling things he shouldn't all over again if he let down his guard.

"She told me that you had job offers from bigger ranches," Nora went on. "And she suspected that you negotiated for this land in exchange for staying."

Easton blinked. She made it sound sordid, somehow, but it wasn't. "Why is it so surprising that I'd be in demand?" he asked. "I run a tight ship. I had offers, that's true. But I didn't strong-arm your dad into changing his will in exchange for sticking around."

"It didn't factor in at all?" Her tone made it clear she wasn't buying that.

"I was offered a position in Idaho for almost twice

what I was making here," he said. "I mentioned it to your dad, but I hadn't even decided if the extra money would be worth it. But that had nothing to do with this house. He said that the house should be lived in, not just sitting there like a relic to days gone by."

"A relic. This is my great-grandparents' house!"

"I wasn't supposed to own it," he retorted. "He wanted me to live in it. I wasn't sure how I felt about that."

"And he decided to just leave it to you in the will?" She shook her head. "These three acres are more precious than the other five hundred ninety-seven. This is where it all started."

And this was the problem—family versus staff. She felt a connection to this land through blood, but for some reason that didn't evolve into actually doing anything. He was an employee here, and he could stay as long as he did his job. Family belonged in a whole different way, but ranches didn't run on sentimental feelings or rightful inheritances—they ran on hard work.

"If you cared about it so much, why didn't you tell him?" Easton retorted. "It isn't my fault you weren't helping out around here. If you showed the least bit of interest in your family's land—and this house—your dad might have done something differently."

"And you're just some innocent bystander who accidentally got some land." Her sarcasm was thick, and his patience was spent.

"All of a sudden I'm some thug, waiting to rob your family of three acres?" he demanded. "I'm the same guy I always was, Nora! You *knew* me! Have I ever been the kind of guy who would manipulate and lie? Cut me some slack!"

"I thought I knew my dad, too!" Her voice quivered and she shook her head, looking away. So that was it—she didn't know what to trust anymore, who was telling her truth. And he couldn't help her. Those were personal issues she'd have to sort out on her own.

"That's the box," he said instead. "I'm not hiding things from you, Nora."

A kind gesture from his boss had turned ugly fast. Her guess was as good as his when it came to why Cliff had done what he did, but he wasn't accepting the blame.

Nora sighed and pulled at the flaps. The boots were on top, and she put them on the floor.

"My mom kept trying to throw these out. They were worn through, and they had no more ankle support…"

She looked at the jacket and put it aside then pulled out the envelope. He knew this was the difficult part. She removed the letters one by one, fanned out the pictures on the floor in front of her. She opened the first letter, read it through, then the second. Easton just watched her.

"He knew about Mia," she said, looking up at Easton.

"Yeah." He wasn't sure what to say to that. This version of his boss—the secretive cheater—didn't sit right with him.

"It doesn't look like Dad and Angela were involved for long."

"That's good news, isn't it?"

"I think so." She pulled a hand through her hair. "I'm taking what I can get at this point. This is not the dad I remember."

"You'd know better than I would," he replied. He might have worked with Cliff, but the man had doted on his daughter. If anyone would have known that softer side of him, it would be Nora.

"He lied to me, too," she said woodenly.

He understood her anger at being lied to, but she didn't understand what utter honesty could get you. His mother had walked out and never once tried to contact him again—that had been honest. His dad had drunk himself into a stupor—that had been a pretty honest reaction, too. He'd have settled for some insincere security from his own parents any day, if it had meant that they'd actually stuck around and been there for him.

"Whatever the fallout," Easton said, "he made his choice—and you won."

Nora was silent for a couple of beats, then she sighed and began to gather the letters and photos back together into one stack.

"You're going to be okay," he said after a moment.

"Do you know that you're the first person to tell me that?" Her expression didn't look convinced. How could anyone comfort Nora in this? She'd lost her dad twice over, and nothing anyone said could make it better.

"And you can't forgive him?" Easton asked.

"I *believed* in him, Easton."

That seemed to be the part that cut her the deepest— she'd been fooled. And now she thought Easton had fooled her, too. But Easton knew he was the one man who hadn't been lying to her. He never had.

Nora pushed herself to her feet and stood there in the lamplight, her eyes clouded with sadness. He wished he could do something, say something, hold her, even, and make this hurt less. He could have been the teenage Easton again, looking at the girl he longed to comfort, knowing that she didn't really want what he had to offer. She wouldn't accept platitudes: *You deserve better.*

And she did deserve better—she always had. She deserved more than a sullied memory of the father she'd adored. She deserved more than the broken, scarred, albeit loyal heart of a man whose own mother hadn't wanted him.

"I'm going to go up to bed," she said after a moment of silence. "I have a doctor's appointment for the babies in the morning, so I'd better get some rest."

"Okay, sure."

She turned and left the room, and he watched her go. The scent of her perfume still hung in the air, as subtle as a memory. The creak of the stairs dissipated overhead. He had some evening chores to check up on, and he was grateful for the excuse to get out, plunge into the fresh air and get away from all of this for a little while. Work—it was cheaper than therapy.

Chapter Seven

The next morning Nora sat in the driver's seat of her truck. The babies were all in their car seats behind her, diapers changed, tummies full. She felt like she'd achieved something, just getting this far. There had been two spit-ups just before leaving, one leaked diaper, Rosie had wanted nothing more than to be cuddled and Bobbie decided that she hated her car seat and didn't want to be strapped in. By the time Nora got them all into the truck, her nerves were frazzled. Now it felt good to just sit in relative silence—the soft sucking of pacifiers soothing her.

Nora had been angry the night before, and that hadn't exactly changed. He said he hadn't used his job offers as any kind of leverage with her dad...was she stupid to believe that? Apparently, she'd lived a lifetime of being altogether too trusting. And when she returned to Hope she'd trusted that Easton would be the same...to never be someone who would hurt her. Someone harmless.

He'd always been quiet, eager to please, willing to step aside for her. Now that she was an adult, she knew she didn't want him constantly giving in to her, but it was possible that she'd still expected it of him. But Easton had grown into a man—strong, resilient, with his own goals and objectives, and he was certainly not harmless anymore. She'd been comfortable feeling a little sorry for him, but she didn't like this new power he seemed to wield around here. And yet, mixed in with all that resentment, she missed him…or what they used to have…the guy who used to sit with her in haylofts and lean against fences as they talked.

Nora turned the key, and the engine moaned and coughed, but didn't turn over. She stopped, frowned then tried again. Nothing.

"Great!" she muttered. This was exactly what she needed. This doctor's appointment was important, and if she couldn't even manage this… She leaned her head against the headrest then heaved a sigh and tried to start the truck again. It ground for a few seconds but didn't start.

The rumble of an engine pulled up behind her, and she looked in the rearview mirror to see Easton. He must be done with his morning work and was back for some coffee. She'd been hoping to be gone by the time he returned. She unrolled her window as he hopped out of his truck and came up beside her.

"Morning," he said. "Everything all right?"

"Not really," she admitted. "I can't start the truck."

"Want me to take a look?"

Even if he got the truck to start, would she make the appointment? She glanced at her watch. "I guess I'll call the doctor's office and say we can't make it."

It was like everything was against her succeeding in one small parenting task this morning. This was the goal for the entire day—go to an appointment. There was nothing else scheduled. Why did it have to be so hard? Was it like this for every mom, or just the wildly inexperienced ones?

Easton crossed his arms and looked away for a moment then nodded toward his vehicle. "Would you rather have a ride into town?"

Right now she didn't really feel like spending any extra time with Easton, but his offer would solve her problem.

"You probably need to eat, and I don't really have time, and if I'm not going to be late, we'd have to leave now," she rambled.

"Let me just clear out the backseat of my cab, and then we can get the car seats moved over," he said.

A kind offer wasn't going to make her trust him again. Regardless, she needed this favor, and she wasn't about to turn it down. Not this morning. If anything, he owed her after whatever he'd done to secure that land—this and so much more.

Ten minutes later they were bumping down the gravel road, past the barn and toward the main drive.

"Thank you," she said as they turned onto the highway. "I appreciate this."

"Sure," he said.

They fell into silence, the only sound the soft sucking of pacifiers from the backseat. It was a forty-minute drive into town, and Nora leaned her head back, watching the looping telephone wires zipping past outside the window.

"Remember that time we rode out past the fields and along the edge of the forest?" Easton asked.

Nora glanced at him. She did. It had been early spring, and she'd asked Easton to go with her. He hadn't wanted to at first because he still had work to do, but then she'd threatened to go alone, and he'd caved in.

"It was fun," she said. "Dad was furious when we got back."

"You were a terrible influence," he said with a teasing smile.

"Oh, I kept your life fun," she countered, chuckling. She'd always known she could convince Easton to do pretty much anything she wanted. All it took was a bat of her lashes. She felt bad about that now.

"You did." The teasing had evaporated from his tone. "Work kept me distracted from home, and you kept me distracted from work. You kept me sane. I ride out to check on fences and cattle, but I don't ride on my days off anymore."

"You should," she said.

"It's different without the company."

He didn't take his eyes off the road. Did he miss her, too? She could remember Easton with those sad eyes. He used to pause in the middle of a chore and look out into space, and she'd always been struck by the depth of sadness in his dark eyes. That had been part of why she liked to drag him away from his duties, because with her he'd laugh. She'd felt like she was rescuing him, saving him from whatever it was that was breaking his heart when he thought no one was looking...

"I was pretty mad last night," Nora said.

"Yeah, I got that."

She glanced over to catch a wry smile on his lips.

"You still mad?" he asked.

"Yes," she said. "I am, but not exclusively at you."

"That's something." He slowed as they came up behind a tractor, signaled and passed it.

"Here's what I want to know," she said. "And honestly. What was there between you and my dad that was so special? And don't say it was nothing, because obviously you were special to him."

Easton was silent for a few beats, then he said, "I didn't take him for granted."

"And I did?" She couldn't hide the irritation that rose at that.

Easton glanced at her and then back to the road. "Of course. He was your dad, and it was perfectly normal to take all that for granted. That's what kids do—they get used to a certain way of living, and they don't stop to think about all that goes into achieving it. That isn't a terrible thing, you know."

"But you were saintly and appreciative," she said, sarcasm edging her tone.

"I wasn't his kid," he retorted. "You're going to inherit all of that land, and I certainly won't. Cliff loved you heart and soul and always would. He was generally fond of me because I'd been around so long and I worked my tail off. There was a massive difference. I wasn't nosing in on your turf."

"That's ironic, because you ended up with my turf."

Easton smiled slightly. "Land isn't love, Nora. It was years of knowing my place. I wanted to learn from your dad, and he liked to teach me stuff. I would do anything extra he asked of me in order to learn. He made me into the professional I am today, and I never took that time with him for granted. Because he *wasn't* my dad."

"And that's why he liked you so much," she clarified.

"I think so," he said. "That and—" He stopped and color crept into his face. For a moment she could see the teenage boy in him again.

"And what?" she pressed.

"It's a little embarrassing," he said, "but he knew how I felt about you." He glanced at her, dark eyes meeting hers, then his gaze snapped back on the road. The moment had been fleeting, but she'd caught something in that eye contact—something deep and warm.

"So you had a crush," she said, trying to sound normal, but she still sounded breathy in her own ears. Bobbie started to whimper, and Nora reached behind her to pop her pacifier back into her mouth.

"It was a weird thing to bond over," Easton admitted. "But I was the one guy who thought you were just as amazing as your dad did."

"I always thought my dad hated the idea of us together," she said. "Anytime he caught us alone, like in the hayloft, he'd blow his top."

"That was then," he said. "After you left, he seemed to change his mind. He never liked the guys you dated, you know."

"They weren't so bad," she countered.

Easton chuckled but didn't answer. She'd known that her dad hated the guys she went out with in Billings. They were the kinds of guys whose boots had never seen mud.

"I kind of knew you had a crush," she admitted. "Kaitlyn thought it was more than that, but I told her it wasn't. You might have to reassure her."

"It was more."

Nora's heart sped up, and she cast about for something to say but couldn't come up with anything. More than a crush…what was that? Love?

"Anyway, after you left, your dad used to joke around that if he had to choose between one of those city slickers and me then he'd take me," Easton said.

"He never told me that." Not directly, at least. Her father had pointed out Easton's work ethic to her more than once. "He's the first one up, and the last one in," her dad had said. "He reminds me of myself when I was his age. You could do worse than finding a man who knows how to work hard, Nora." Was giving Easton the house her father's way of "handpicking" her husband? That wasn't really Cliff's style.

"Look, it was nice to have your dad's respect," Easton said. "But I wasn't the kind of guy who could be led to water, either. Regardless of how I felt about you. I respected your dad, and I appreciated all he did for me, but I make my own life choices."

"So you didn't really want anything more with me—" She didn't know what she was fishing for here—absolution, maybe?

"I didn't want to be the guy always chasing at your heels," he replied. "What I felt for you was considerably more than a crush, but I didn't want to chase you down and try to convince you I was worth your time. If you didn't know it yet, then that ship had sailed. I put my energy into getting over you instead."

"Pragmatic..." She swallowed.

"Always." He laughed softly, and her heart squeezed at the sound of it. He was every inch a man now, and it was a whole lot harder to ignore. But he'd made the right choice in getting over her.

"So you think Dad wanted us to get together," she clarified.

"I don't really think it matters what he wanted now," Easton said frankly. "He's gone."

Gone with her father were the days when Easton could be talked into horseback riding, and that was probably for the best.

"You're right," she admitted. "I might be able to pick that bone with him if he were still alive, but he's not."

Easton glanced toward her again, and she could see the warmth in his gaze—something that smoldered deeper. It wasn't the same shy look from years ago when he'd had a crush. This was the steady gaze of a man—unwavering, direct, knowledgeable.

He didn't say anything, though, and neither did she.

EASTON PARKED IN front of the two-story building that housed the doctor's office. It took a few minutes to get the babies out of the truck, and then Nora carried two car seats and he carried Rosie's into the waiting room. While Nora went to tell the receptionist that they'd arrived, Easton glanced around at the people seated in the chairs that edged the room. He nodded to two men he knew, and a couple of older ladies looked from the car seats to Nora and then up at Easton, their expressions filled with questions and dirty laundry, no doubt.

Easton glanced at his watch, wondering how long this appointment would take. They were getting low on calf formula. He could let Nora call him on his cell when she was done, and he could head down to the ranch and feed shop... Rosie started to fuss, and Nora glanced back at him. She looked overwhelmed by all of this, and he felt a tickle of sympathy.

"Do you mind?" she asked hopefully.

Easton unbuckled Rosie from her car seat and picked her up. That settled the infant immediately, and she snuggled into his arms, big brown eyes blinking up at him. Rosie definitely liked to be held. Bobbie and Riley were asleep in their seats, and Nora was rooting through her purse for something. He wasn't getting out of here anytime soon, was he?

"They're very cute," one of the older ladies said, putting down her copy of *Reader's Digest*. She had short, permed hair that was dyed something close to black. It made her face look pale and older than she probably was.

Easton used his boot to move the car seat toward a line of free chairs then sat down in one of them. The woman scooted over, peering into Rosie's tiny face.

"These are...the ones..." She looked at Easton meaningfully. Had gossip really gone around town so fast that people he didn't even recognize were asking about the situation? He decided to play dumb and hope she took the hint.

"They're cute all right," he said.

"But these are Cliff Carpenter's grandchildren, right?" she plowed on. "These are the babies with that poor, poor mother…"

He closed his eyes for a moment, looking for calm. "It's private," he said, trying to sound more polite than he felt right now.

"I never imagined," she went on. "My husband did some mechanic work for him on the tractors—you know, when it got beyond what they could handle on site—so I knew Cliff pretty well. And he just seemed so devoted to Dina. So devoted. Just…" She shook her head, searching for words.

"Devoted," Easton said drily. Why was he encouraging this?

"Yes!" she exclaimed. "He really was. He talked about her all the time, and he only ever mentioned his daughter—I mean the *local* daughter. He never, ever mentioned anyone *else*, if you know what I mean. If he had, I might have said something, but he never did. I wouldn't have guessed if those babies hadn't arrived."

She straightened, looking up guiltily as Nora came in their direction, a car seat in each hand. Nora sank into the chair next to Easton and nodded to the woman.

"Hi, Ethel," Nora said.

"Morning," Ethel murmured, but her gaze moved over the babies, her mouth drawn together in a little pucker of judgment.

"I never knew," Ethel said, leaning forward again. "Just so you know, Nora, I never knew."

Nora cast Ethel a withering look—apparently she

was past polite at this point, and Easton had to choke back a smile.

"If I had, I would have said something, too," Ethel went on, not to be dissuaded. "I side with the women. How many times have we been tilled under by a man with a wandering eye? So I wouldn't have kept a secret like that. I'd have spoken up, and let him face the music. That's what I'd have done."

"It's a sensitive topic, ma'am," Easton said quietly.

"I'd say it is!" she retorted. "My sister married a man who couldn't keep it in his pants, so I know exactly how sensitive these things can be. It is amazing what some men do with their free time. My sister's husband didn't even try to be faithful. He slept with everyone within reach, and she knew it, but she wasn't about to give him his walking papers, either. It's all well and good to tell her that she should kick him out, but it was her life, and her marriage, and I couldn't interfere now, could I?"

"Hardly," Easton said wryly, but she didn't seem to read his tone, because she kept talking.

"Everyone in her town knew that her husband had fathered two other children. In fact, I attended the wedding of one of those girls. My sister's husband wasn't there, of course, because he was still pretending that he wasn't her daddy, but I was a friend of a friend, so I went to that wedding. I wasn't invited to the reception, but—"

"Ethel," Nora said, shooting a dangerously sweet smile in the older woman's direction. "Shut up."

Ethel blinked, color rising in her cheeks, and she

YOUR PARTICIPATION IS REQUESTED!

Dear Reader,

Since you are a lover of our books – we would like to get to know you!

Inside you will find a short Reader's Survey. Sharing your answers with us will help our editorial staff understand who you are and what activities you enjoy.

To thank you for your participation, we would like to send you 2 books and 2 gifts – **ABSOLUTELY FREE!**

Enjoy your gifts with our appreciation,

Pam Powers

**SEE INSIDE
FOR READER'S
SURVEY**

For Your Reading Pleasure...

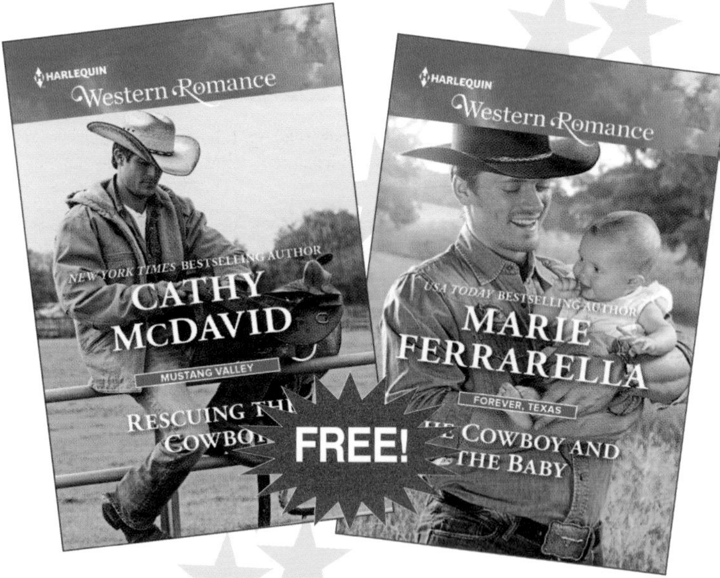

We'll send you 2 books and 2 gifts
ABSOLUTELY FREE
just for completing our Reader's Survey!

YOURS FREE!
We'll send you two fabulous surprise gifts absolutely FREE, just for trying our books!

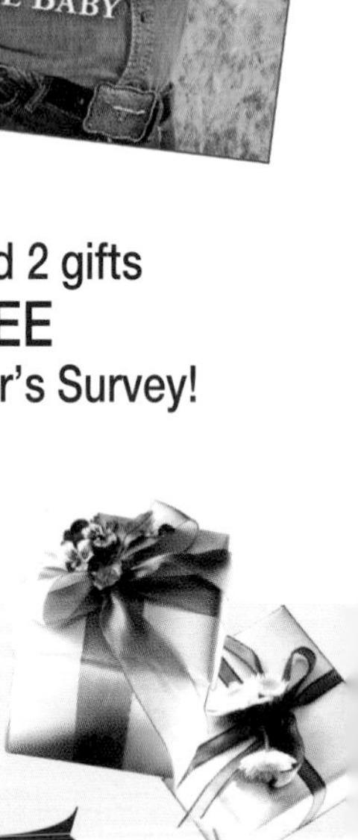

Visit us at:
www.ReaderService.com

YOUR READER'S SURVEY
"THANK YOU" FREE GIFTS INCLUDE:
- ▶ 2 FREE books
- ▶ 2 lovely surprise gifts

▶ DETACH AND MAIL CARD TODAY! ▶

PLEASE FILL IN THE CIRCLES COMPLETELY TO RESPOND

1) What type of fiction books do you enjoy reading? (Check all that apply)
- ○ Suspense/Thrillers
- ○ Action/Adventure
- ○ Modern-day Romances
- ○ Historical Romance
- ○ Humor
- ○ Paranormal Romance

2) What attracted you most to the last fiction book you purchased on impulse?
- ○ The Title
- ○ The Cover
- ○ The Author
- ○ The Story

3) What is usually the greatest influencer when you <u>plan</u> to buy a book?
- ○ Advertising
- ○ Referral
- ○ Book Review

4) How often do you access the internet?
- ○ Daily
- ○ Weekly
- ○ Monthly
- ○ Rarely or never

5) How many NEW paperback fiction novels have you purchased in the past 3 months?
- ○ 0 - 2
- ○ 3 - 6
- ○ 7 or more

YES! I have completed the Reader's Survey. Please send me the 2 FREE books and 2 FREE gifts (gifts are worth about $10 retail) for which I qualify. I understand that I am under no obligation to purchase any books, as explained on the back of this card.

154/354 HDL GLNW

FIRST NAME

LAST NAME

ADDRESS

APT.#

CITY

STATE/PROV.

ZIP/POSTAL CODE

WR-217-SUR17

opened her mouth to say something then shut it with a click.

"Ethel Carmichael," the receptionist called. "The doctor is ready for you now."

Ethel rose to her feet and stalked toward the hallway in time for Easton to overhear the nurse say something about taking her blood pressure. They might want to wait on that to get a normal reading, he thought, and when he glanced over at Nora, she sent him a scathing look.

"What?" he asked.

She rolled her eyes and looked away. This one wasn't his fault. Ethel was the storyteller. Women like Ethel had memories like elephants for juicy gossip, but looking down into Rosie's tiny face, the humor in the situation bled away.

This baby girl—and her sisters—would experience the kind of sympathetic tut-tutting that he had for most of his growing-up years. Easton had enough scandal surrounding his own parentage, and he knew what it felt like to have every woman in town look at him with sympathy because his mother had walked out on him. That kind of stigma clung like a skunk's spray.

When Easton was in the fifth grade, they were supposed to make key chains for their mothers for Mother's Day. Easton had dutifully made that key chain, braiding leather strips as they were instructed. All he'd wanted was to blend in with the class, but that never happened. The other kids whispered about him—he didn't have a mom to give the gift to—and the teacher was extra nice to him, which he'd pay for at recess time. So he'd finished his key chain and in the place where they were supposed to write "I love you, Mom," he'd written something profoundly dirty instead. He wanted to change that look of pity he saw into something else—anger, preferably.

It worked, and every Mother's Day afterward, he pulled the same trick, because things like Mother's Day couldn't be avoided. These girls would have the same problem, except for them it would be at the mention of grandparents, and everyone would clam up and look at them with high-handed sympathy. And they'd hate it—he could guarantee that. With any luck, they would find something better than profanity as a distraction.

Hang in there, kiddo, he thought as he looked down into Rosie's wide-eyed face. She flailed a small arm then yawned. He couldn't say it would get better, because it wouldn't. But she'd get used to it.

Chapter Eight

That evening Easton stood over the open hood of Nora's truck where it had stalled out in front of his house. It needed a part—one he could swap out of another Chevy that was parked in a shed. The truck would be up and running in no time. He'd get the part tomorrow during his workday and fix her vehicle the next evening. Lickety-split.

The sun was sinking in the west, shadows lengthening and birds twittering their evening songs. He liked this time of day; after his work was done he had the satisfaction of having accomplished something. That was what he loved about this job—yeah, there was always more to do the next day, but a day's work meant something. He'd been thinking about that trip to the doctor's office with the babies earlier that afternoon, and he couldn't quite sort out his feelings. Truth was, he felt protective of those little tykes, but that didn't sit right with him. He wasn't supposed to be getting attached.

Their ride home from town had been quiet. He'd wanted to say something—he knew Nora was upset about Ethel Carmichael's attempt at conversation, but she'd probably be in for a whole lot more of that. People had known Cliff, loved him, which meant he'd left more than just Dina and Nora stunned by the truth. And in spite of it all, Easton still felt like he owed his late boss something more—a defense, maybe. He just didn't know how.

A cool breeze felt good against his face and arms. The bugs were out—he slapped a mosquito on his wrist. Easton wiped his hands on a rag then flicked off the light that hung from the hood of Nora's truck, unhooked it and banged the hood shut. Above him, a window scraped open and he looked up.

Nora stood, framed between billowing white curtains, and she lifted her hand in a silent wave. She looked so sweet up there, her skin bathed in golden sunlight, her sun-streaked hair tumbling down around her shoulders. Her nose and cheeks looked a little burned, and squinting up at her like that, he couldn't help but notice just how gorgeous she was.

"Hey," he said.

"I just got the babies to sleep," she said. "Are you fixing my truck?"

"Yup." He turned his attention to rubbing the last of the grease out of the lines in his palm. "But I won't be done until tomorrow."

"Thank you." She brushed her hair out of her face and leaned her elbows onto the windowsill. "You don't have to do that, you know."

"Yeah?" he retorted. "You gonna do it?"

It was a challenge. She'd never been one to tinker

with an engine, and he'd fixed her ride more than once when they were teenagers.

"I'd call a garage."

A garage. Yeah, right. A garage was for quitters. Any cowboy with a lick of self-respect knew how to fix his truck, and only when it was halfway flattened did he lower himself to calling in a mechanic.

"You're going to be my boss one day," he said. "I might as well make nice now."

She rolled her eyes. "We'll be in our sixties by then."

She had a point. It'd likely be years before her mother grew too feeble to actually run this place. And she'd told him before that she wasn't living for a funeral. But if she settled down with her mom at the main house, he'd be fixing her truck for a long time to come as her employee. Did he mind that?

"You should stick around," he said, shooting her a grin. "You'd enjoy fighting with me more often."

"I thought you said you'd make nice," she countered.

"Yeah, how long can that last?" he asked with a low laugh. "I'm not sixteen anymore, Nora."

She raised an eyebrow. "Me, neither."

Then she disappeared from the window. He stood there, looking up at the billowing curtains for a moment before he smiled to himself and scrubbed his hand once more with the rag. Some things didn't change, like the way Nora could fix him to the spot with a single look… but she was no teen angel anymore. She was a grown woman, with a woman's body and a woman's direct gaze. He wasn't a kid anymore, either, and he wasn't at her beck and call. This had been about his job—a truck on this ranch that needed work. That was it.

The drive into town—okay that had been more than official duties around here, but he and Nora had some history. She'd always be special to him. Didn't they say that a first love was never fully erased? Something like that. She'd been part of his formative years.

Easton's cell phone rang, and he glanced at the number before picking it up.

"Dad?"

"Hi." His dad's voice sounded tight, and sober for a change. "What are you up to?"

"Working."

"Well…take a break. You need to come over."

"Why?" Easton looked at his watch. "It's not a good time, Dad. I have to get up early. You know that."

"You'll want to come by, son," his father said. "There's someone you'll want to see."

"Yeah?" He wasn't convinced. "Who?"

"Your mom."

Easton froze, the rag falling from his hand and landing in the gravel. He tried to swallow but couldn't. A cold sweat erupted on his forehead, and the breeze suddenly felt chilly.

"Ha," he said, forcing the word out. "Not funny. Actually, kind of mean."

"I'm not joking," his father said. "I'm looking at her right now. If you wanted to see her, now's the time."

"Okay," he said, his heart banging in his chest. "I'll be there in fifteen minutes."

Hanging up the phone, he fished his keys out of

his pocket and headed for his own vehicle. Mom was back? Was Dad hallucinating? Maybe he'd widened his addictive repertoire to include some drug use. Easton scrubbed a hand through his hair and hauled open the door. He had to stop and suck in a few deep breaths because his hands were trembling. There was something in his dad's voice that told him this was no joke.

After twenty years' absence, what could she possibly want? After missing his childhood…after letting him grow up with a drunk of a father and a hole in his heart the size of Wisconsin, what brought her back to Hope?

NORA LOOKED OUT the window in time to see Easton's truck back out of the drive then take off down the gravel road, leaving a billow of dust behind him.

That's weird, she thought. Where was he off to in such a hurry?

Maybe an evening to herself was better anyway. Flirting with Easton hadn't really been part of the plan, yet she kept finding herself doing it. Was it habit? A throwback from her teenage years? Or maybe she missed all the control she used to have—a boy following after her who'd do anything she asked.

"I'm not that shallow," she muttered to herself.

Her day had been tiring. The doctor's appointment itself had been routine. The babies had been weighed, measured and declared to be healthy. It was that encounter with Ethel Carmichael that had gotten to her. It was only an old woman's gossipy streak, she told herself. Nora shouldn't worry about it…but she did.

She sighed and rubbed her hands over her face. Hope, Montana, was a nice town—friendly, helpful, attractive—but it was also a town where not too much happened. Everybody knew everybody else, or just about, and half the town was related to each other by marriage. People remembered each other's stories because they were a part of each other's lives. And when people saw the girls in Beauty's Ice Cream Shop or saw them in church, they'd think of Cliff and the scandal around the triplets' arrival. These things didn't just go away.

Nora could handle some gossip. But these three little girls deserved a happy life. What options did Nora have? She could stay in Hope where the girls would have a distanced grandmother they weren't allowed to call "Grandma," and where the story of their grandfather's infidelity would follow them everywhere they went. That was assuming that Nora could make a life here—get a job, find a place that didn't cost too much... maybe with enough family about, she'd be able to pull together a decent life for the girls, financially, at least.

Or she could go back to Billings where she'd have to drop them off at day care every day...and maybe get a second job doing some contract bookkeeping to be able to afford that. They'd have a tired, overworked mom who did her best to keep up with everything. They wouldn't have many new clothes or the toys they wanted. There wouldn't be summer vacations, unless you counted coming back to Hope where everyone would look at them sideways and the girls still couldn't call their grandmother "Grandma."

Or—and this was the option that brought a lump to her throat—she could accept that she couldn't provide the kind of life that these babies deserved. She couldn't give them a comfortable home with a bedroom for each of them, or summer vacations, or new clothes. She couldn't even provide a stable family life to make up for those other things. She wasn't married. There would be no dad to give them that important male influence in their lives. There wouldn't even be a doting grandma to cuddle them and tell them stories about their family. And she'd never make this town look past the scandal the triplets' grandfather created...

Nora sank onto the side of her bed, her heart sodden with anxiety. That was what the visit to the doctor's office had shown her—she could provide the basics, but she couldn't shield them from the rest. And if there was a family out there that would adopt these girls together, love them and celebrate them, provide birthday parties and new shoes... If there were adoptive grandparents who would make cookies with them and read them stories, look them in the eye and tell them how loved and wanted they were... Could she really deny these little girls that kind of life?

Nora looked through the bars of the crib at the sleeping babies. Their lashes brushed their plump cheeks; their hair swirled across their heads in damp curls. Bobbie was making phantom sucking noises, her little tongue poked out of her mouth, and Riley let out a soft sigh in her sleep. Nora put a finger in Rosie's tiny hand, and she clamped down on it.

"I love you," she whispered.

It was true—she'd fallen in love with her girls, and if money didn't matter or if she could wave a magic wand and make everyone forget the pain associated with these children, she'd raise them herself and be their mom. But money did matter, and so did scandal. They were brand-new to this world, and already they were steeped in it. She was the one Mia had designated as their provider, and she had to do what was best for the babies.

A tear slipped down Nora's cheek, and she wiped it away with her free hand. She gently stroked Rosie's soft fingers, inhaling the delicate smell of sleeping infants. She'd remember this, cherish it always. She wasn't their mother—Mia was. Nora was an in-between person who had to give them her heart in order to take care of them. But she couldn't keep them, no matter how much her heart broke at the thought of letting go.

When she'd taken the babies from the hospital, they'd given her some business cards from social workers and adoption agencies. She'd shoved them into her wallet and forgotten about them, but she knew what she'd have to do.

Tomorrow. Not tonight. Tonight she had to let herself feel this pain and have a good cry. Then in the morning she'd call an adoption agency and see what kinds of options the girls might have.

Chapter Nine

Easton's father, Mike Ross, lived at the end of Hunter Street. There were no shade trees, just brown lawns and old houses—several of which were empty. The Ross house was at the end of the road before asphalt simply evaporated into scrub grass. A couple of cars were on blocks in the front yard, and a chain and a massive dog bowl sat abandoned by the front door. The dog had died years ago, but the reminder of his presence seemed to help keep thieves and religious proselytizers at bay. Which was good when it came to thieves, but in Easton's humble opinion, a little religion wouldn't hurt his old man.

When Easton pulled into the driveway behind a red SUV, all those old feelings of anger and resentment settled back onto his shoulders, too. This was why he never came home—it reminded him of things he'd rather leave in the past. Like constantly feeling like a failure no matter what he did, and acting rough and angry to get away from the pity.

Except he'd longed for his mom every day since she'd left, imagined ways she might return, set scenes in his mind when she'd see him as a grown man and her heart would fill with pride. Those had been fantasies, because her actually coming back would solidify the fact that she'd been able to return all along and had chosen not to.

He sat in his truck for a couple of minutes, his hands on the steering wheel in a white-knuckled grip. That was probably her SUV, all new and shiny. So she had enough money for that. Maybe she'd stayed away for the same reasons he did now—because she didn't like to remember. He undid his seat belt and got out of the truck.

The front door was never used; in fact, his dad had a bunch of junk piled in front of it from the inside. Easton angled around to the side door. He didn't bother knocking, just opened it. The kitchen was smoky from his father's cigarettes, so Easton left the door open to let it clear a bit.

"Hello?" he called.

A woman emerged from the living room—slim, made up, wearing a pair of jeans and a light blouse. Her hair was dyed brown now, cut short but stylish. Her face was the same face he remembered, though. Even that one crooked tooth when she smiled hesitantly.

"Easton?" she whispered.

"Mom." Tears welled up in his eyes, and he stood there looking at her awkwardly.

"Oh, sweetheart—" She came forward as if to hug him, but he didn't move into it, so she ended up patting his arm a few times. She looked up into his face, and he could see that she'd aged. She was no longer the woman in her early twenties matching his dad drink for drink—she would be forty-seven this year. He'd done the math.

"So—" He cleared his throat. "Where've you been?"

"Can I hug you?" she asked softly.

"Not right now." If he let her hug him, the tears he'd been holding back for years would start, and he couldn't let that happen. He could cry later, alone, but not in front of her. He needed answers.

His father came into the room and scraped back a kitchen chair. He was thin and tall, lined and slightly yellowed from nicotine.

"Should we sit?" she asked cautiously. "Just come sit with me, son."

He followed her to the flier-strewn table and sat opposite her. She looked him over then reached out and put her hand on top of his.

"You look good," she said. "Really good."

"Thanks." He pulled his hand back as the tears started to rise inside his chest. "You look like you're not doing too badly for yourself. What took so long to come see how I was doing?"

"I wanted to—" She looked toward his father. "I talked to your dad on the phone a few times, and he said you were doing really well. He said if I came around I'd ruin things for you."

"What?" Easton darted a disgusted look at his old man. "And you believed that lying sack of—" He bit off the last word and sucked in a shaky breath. Profanity was a bit of a habit when he felt cornered. *"You left me."*

And suddenly, he was nothing more than an eight-year-old boy again, staring at the mom who was supposed to be better at this. In that note she'd left on the fridge, she hadn't said anything loving. Her last words had been "He's your problem now." She'd ditched him, left town, and while he'd squirmed his way around those words over the years, trying to apply different meaning to them that would still allow her to return for him, looking at his mother now brought the words back like a punch in the gut.

"I know..." She blinked a few times then licked her lips. "I was young when I had you—seventeen, if you remember. I didn't know how to deal with everything. I was so overwhelmed..."

"Except you weren't seventeen when you left. You were twenty-five. That's a solid adult."

"Yes." She didn't offer any excuses.

"And the note—"

"I wasn't in a good place when I scratched that out," she interrupted. "I don't remember exactly what I said."

"I do." Easton glanced at his old man. His dad would remember that note, too. "You said you were sick of this life and I was Dad's problem from then on."

She winced. "I didn't mean—"

"Sure you did. Or you would have come back."

She swallowed, glanced at his father. What was she looking for, some kind of united front?

"So you figured you'd leave me with him." Easton jutted a thumb toward his father. "He was a more suitable parent?"

"He had the house," she said. "I just drove away one

day. I wasn't thinking about the future—just about getting some space." She was quiet for a moment. "And I knew I wasn't much of a mom."

Yeah, that was evident. With her sitting in front of him, he was able to separate the fantasies of the gentle mother stroking his hair from the reality of the emotionally distant mother who'd spent hours a day smoking in this very kitchen.

"I tried to see you," she added.

"When?" he demanded. He found that hard to believe.

"The summer you were fourteen. I was in the area and I called your dad. He said he got you a job at a local ranch and you were doing really well. He said you were happy, and you didn't remember me."

"*You* said that?" Easton glared at his father across the table. "I was happy, was I? I didn't need her?"

His father shrugged. "We did okay. She's the one who left."

That had been his father's mantra over the years— she was the one who left, as if all their problems had been caused by the one who walked away instead of the parents who hadn't done their job to begin with.

Easton turned back to his mother. "I was doing okay because Cliff Carpenter hired me and took over where Dad left off. I wasn't happy. I was making do. And Dad didn't get me anything. I waited outside the ranch and feed store and asked every single rancher that came and left if he'd hire me. Cliff was the only one to say yes. Dad didn't do squat for me. He drank every day, ran this house into the ground and smacked me around if I was within reach."

"Hey—" his father started.

"Shut up, Dad." Easton wasn't in any mood to argue about facts with his old man, and his father seemed to sense that, because he subsided back into a brooding silence.

"I—" His mother swallowed hard and dropped her gaze. "I didn't know all that."

"I'm a ranch manager now," he added. "I own my own home. I have a life, and I steer clear of this dump."

"Maybe I could—"

"No!" He knew what she was about to ask—to see the life he'd built for himself. And while he'd dreamed of that opportunity since he was eight years old, he realized that he didn't actually want it now. She didn't deserve to feel better about how he'd turned out. He wanted to hurt her back—make her feel the rejection he'd felt his entire life. "You aren't welcome in my home."

They fell into silence for a few beats. He could take all his pain and anguish out on her, or he could get some of those answers at last.

"So what have you been doing all these years?" Easton asked. "You're dressed pretty well."

"I'm—" She looked down at her hands splayed on the tabletop, and his eye followed hers to the wedding ring. "I'm married again. His name is Tom. He's very sweet. I'm a recovering alcoholic, so I don't drink. It took a few years of hard work, but I got there."

"So where'd you find...Tom...then?" The name tasted sour on his tongue.

"Church," she replied. "We've been married sixteen years now. He's a good man."

Sixteen years of marriage, and she'd stayed away from him. There had been a home she could have brought him to, a cupboard full of food... He did the mental math, and he'd been twelve when she'd gotten married—plenty of time to have given him some sort of childhood.

"What does Tom do?"

"He's an electrician."

Blast it—so normal and balanced. His mom walked away and got to marry some utterly normal Tom, afford new clothes—something he'd never had growing up— and drive a new SUV... And he'd been left in addiction-induced poverty, dreaming of some fantasy mother.

"Where do you live?" he asked.

"Billings."

"Three hours away?" he asked incredulously. "I was here missing you, longing for my mom to come back for me, and all that time you were a mere three hours from here?"

Easton rubbed his hands over his face. He'd dreamed of a chance to see his mother again, to try to mend this jagged hole in his heart that she'd left behind. Some days he wanted answers, and other days he wanted comfort. Today he had the chance to hug her and he couldn't bring himself to do it. He was finally face-to-face with his mom again, and he felt something he'd never expected—he hated her.

"I'm so sorry—" Her voice shook and she wiped a tear from her cheek. "I thought you were doing well, that if I came back I'd ruin things for you. I was so ashamed of the woman I used to be. I was mean, drunk most of the time and just a shell of a person…" She shook her head. "I thought you'd remember all of that."

"Not really," he admitted. "A bit, I mean. But I was young. I think Dad remembered that more. I…uh…I kept your Led Zeppelin T-shirt under my mattress. I remembered the smell of your cigarettes in the morning, and the sound of your laughter."

"My T-shirt—" The look on her face was like he'd punched her with those words.

"It helped me sleep sometimes." Why was he telling her this? Blast it, his complaints made him sound like a whimpering puppy! He wasn't meaning to open up, but he'd been holding all of this in for so long…

"I wasn't sure you'd *want* me back."

"Not sure I do now, either," he snapped. That was half of a lie. He did want her back, but he also wanted her to pay for her absence. He wanted her to feel some of what she'd done to him. "So why now?"

"I don't know," she said quietly. "I got into my vehicle and started driving. I called Tom from the road and said I was coming to see my son. I need to go back tonight, but I had to see you again. I missed you so much."

"Not enough to drive the three hours before this," he pointed out.

"I wanted to…" She swallowed hard. "I couldn't

shake the guilt of having left you like I did. Then Brandon had his eighth birthday…"

"Brandon?" he asked slowly. "Who's that?"

"My son—your half brother…" She grabbed her purse from the back of her chair and rummaged through it. She pulled out a school photo and pushed it across the table toward him. Easton didn't touch it, but he looked at the smiling face of a kid with dirty-blond hair and a lopsided grin. *Her son.*

Easton's stomach dropped as the reality of this moment settled into his gut. She'd gotten married, had another little boy and she'd been the mom she should have been to Easton to this other kid.

"So…" Easton's voice shook. "I have a half brother."

"Yes." She nodded, a tentative smile coming to her lips. "And he's a sweet boy. I know you'd like him. He's got such a big heart."

"And you've been there for him," Easton clarified, his voice firming up as rage coursed through him. "You've taken him to soccer practice and given him birthday parties…hell, even birthday presents?"

"He likes chess, actually, but—" She stopped, sensing where he was going with this. "I was older. I was wiser. There's enough money now—"

Easton let out a string of expletives and rose to his feet, the chair underneath him clattering to the floor.

"You were my *mother*!" he roared.

She sat in stunned silence, and his father shuffled his feet against the crumb-laden floor. Easton stared down at the parents who'd brought him into this world and then failed to provide for him. He couldn't stop the tears anymore—he was blinded by them. His shoulders shook and he turned away, trying to get some sort of control over himself, but now that it had started, he couldn't seem to dam it up. He slammed a hand against the wall then leaned there as he sobbed.

He felt his mother's arms wrap around him from behind, and she shook with tears, too.

"Damn it, Mom, I hate you," he wept.

"I know," she whispered. "I know…"

Then he turned around, and for the first time since he was eight years old, he wrapped his arms around his mom and hugged her. He hugged her tighter than was probably comfortable, but she didn't complain, and he didn't dare let go.

She'd learned how to be a mother after all, but she'd learned with somebody else. And that didn't do a thing for Easton. He'd already grown up, and he'd done it without a mom.

Nora stood in the kitchen mixing baby formula at the counter. She shook up the third bottle, watching the bubbles form. She was getting used to this hour, and she woke up before her cell phone alarm now. It was midnight, and she was in her white cotton nightgown, the cool night air winding around her bare legs. It was strange, but this house, which had always been so firmly *hers* in her heart, felt empty without Easton in it. He'd driven off that evening, and he hadn't come back.

Earlier that evening, her mother had asked if she'd come for lunch at the house. She was having Nora's aunt and uncle come over, and she needed some moral support. This was Cliff's sister and her husband—both of whom had been close with Cliff.

"They'll want to meet the babies, too, I'm sure," her mother had said. "They're Cliff's grandkids, after all."

There weren't going to be any easy explanations, no simple family relationships for these girls. And they needed family—the supportive, loving kind, not the backbiting, gossiping kind. Nora needed to know now if that was even a possibility after what her father had done. She was willing to look into adoptive options for the girls, but she hadn't fully committed to it—not yet. Other single mothers managed it—pulled it all together on their own—but *how*?

Normally at this time of year, the Carpenters hosted a corn roast and barbecue for family and friends, also as a way to thank the staff for their hard work over the summer. She'd asked her mother if she wanted to go ahead with it this year, but with Cliff's death and the subsequent drama, it hardly seemed like a priority.

Standing in the kitchen at midnight, Nora put down the last bottle of formula. She'd considered calling Easton's cell phone a couple of times, but hadn't. This was her problem to untangle on her own, and while a listening ear might be comforting, no one else could give her the answer. Besides, it wasn't Easton's job to listen to her go on about her problems. He had problems of his own. But would it be too much to ask of a friend?

As she gathered up the bottles, a truck's engine rumbled up the drive. She felt a wave of relief. Why she should feel this way, she didn't know, but perhaps it was just old habits dying hard—tough times nudging her toward Easton. She really wanted to talk to him about the girls—but more than that, she wanted to hear what he had to say about them. It would help her hammer out her own feelings out loud with another person who wouldn't judge her, because Heaven knew she was judging herself pretty harshly right now.

The back door opened and Easton stepped inside. His shoulders were slumped, and his face looked puffy and haggard. If she didn't know him better, she'd think he'd been crying. He didn't look up at her as he kicked off his boots and hung his hat on the peg.

"Easton? Oh my goodness, are you all right?"

He scrubbed a hand through his hair. "Yeah, I'm fine."

"No, you're not!" She crossed the kitchen and caught his arm on his way past. "Look at me."

He turned toward her and she could see the red rims of his eyes, the same old sadness welling up in his dark gaze. "My mom came back."

Nora stared at him. A slew of questions cascaded through her mind, but they swept past as she saw the pain etched in Easton's features.

"She was at my dad's place."

Nora's breath came out in a rush and she looked from Easton to the bottles and then back at her friend again. His mom—she knew what this meant…or at the very least she knew how heavily this would have hit him.

"I need to feed the babies," she said quietly. "You want to help? We could talk…"

He was silent for a beat, and she half expected him to say no, that he was fine, and to go up and lock himself into his bedroom.

"Sure," he said.

She picked up the bottles from the counter and they moved together toward the stairs.

"What happened, exactly?" she asked as they climbed the narrow staircase. "Is she still here?"

"She's left already—for Billings. She's been there this whole time. She's remarried with another kid."

His voice was low and wooden as he went over what had happened tonight. Nora picked up Riley and passed her to Easton. He was more practiced now in handling babies, and he took the infant easily. His expression softened as he looked down into the sleeping face.

"They're so little," he said quietly. He teased the bottle's nipple between her lips. Nora scooped up Rosie and let Bobbie sleep for another few minutes. "Can you imagine anyone just walking away?"

Tears misted her eyes. Wasn't that exactly what she was considering with the triplets? Was she just as bad as Easton's mother? Or had Easton's mother done the best that she could under the circumstances? Maybe she just wanted to excuse Easton's mom because it would make her look infinitely better by comparison.

"How do you feel now that you've seen her again?" Nora asked quietly.

"Conflicted," he admitted. "I've wanted this for years—a chance to see her, to hug her again—and now that I have it, I'm filled with rage."

"You're probably in shock," she said.

"I spent years loving her in spite of her faults." He heaved a sigh. "But she figured out how to be a decent parent when she had her second child—Brandon. I saw a picture. Cute kid. And all I could feel was anger. That's awful, isn't it? He's just some kid. Do I really want him to suffer like I did?"

She didn't respond, and the only sound in the room was that of the babies drinking their bottles.

"She wants me to meet him," Easton said after a moment.

"Do you want to?" Nora asked.

"I don't know. Not really. Yes." He shook his head. "You know what I want? I want to go back in time and have her be there for me, too. She takes Brandon to chess club three times a week, and she drives him to birthday parties. She's a stay-at-home mom." He muttered an oath then looked sheepishly at Nora. "Riley'll never remember that."

Nora smiled. "She'll be fine."

Easton jiggled the bottle to get Riley drinking again and adjusted her position, then he continued, "My mom said she wanted to be home for Brandon, because her husband works long hours, and he needs someone to talk about his school day with. Talk about his school day! What I would've given for my mom to just sit and listen to me for a few minutes."

"Will you see her again?" she asked.

"She'll come back again on Saturday afternoon. She'll text me the details."

Nora tipped Rosie up against her shoulder and patted her back. Easton did the same with Riley. From the crib, Bobbie was starting to squirm in her sleep, probably feeling hungry. Riley burped, and Easton wiped her mouth with a cloth, then laid her back down in the crib. He picked up Bobbie next. When had he gotten so good at this?

"Should I feed her?" he asked.

Rosie hadn't burped yet, and Nora nodded. Easton grabbed the third bottle and Bobbie immediately started slurping it back.

"It's funny—I have her cell number. I could call her if I wanted to… I could text my mom. How many times have I wished I could contact her—say something to her? Now I could…with a text." A smile creased his tired face. "That's something, isn't it?"

And in those shining eyes, she saw the boy she used to know, who would sit next to her in the hayloft, listening to her go on about her small and insignificant problems. He hadn't mentioned his mother often back then, but she could remember one time when he'd said, "When my mom comes back, I'm going to buy her a house."

"A house?" she'd asked. "How will you do that? Houses cost more than you've got."

"In three years I'll be eighteen. I'll drop out of school and work full-time," he'd replied. "And then we'll live in that house together, and my dad can rot by himself. I'll take care of her."

He'd always planned for his mother's return. Somehow he'd been convinced that she'd come back, and he'd been right. Except when they were kids, he'd been certain that she'd need him.

They resettled the babies into the crib, but they stayed there in the darkness, standing close enough together that she could feel the warmth of his body radiating against hers.

"The one thing she didn't tell me—" His voice broke. "She never said why she left me behind."

She couldn't see him well enough in the dim light, but she could hear that rasp of deep emotion against his iron reserve. That was a wound that wouldn't heal.

"Easton…"

She wrapped her arms around his waist and leaned her cheek against his broad chest. He slipped his muscular arms around her and she could feel his cheek rest on the top of her head. He smelled good—musky, with a hint of hay. His body was roped with muscle, and he leaned into her, his body warming her in a way that felt intimate and pleading.

Neither of them spoke, and he leaned down farther, wrapping his arms around her a little more closely, tugging her against him more firmly. She could feel the thud of his heartbeat against her chest, and she closed her eyes, breathing in his manly scent. Somehow all either of them seemed to want was to be closer, to absorb all of each other's pain into their bodies and share it.

Easton pulled back and she found her face inches from his, and his dark eyes moved over her face. She could see the faint freckles across his cheekbones, the soft shadow of his stubble veiling a few acne scars. He was the same old Easton, all grown up, and while she could still see the sweet boy in those dark eyes, she could also see the rugged man—the survivor, the cowboy—and the intensity of that gaze also reminded her that he was very capable of being so much more than that...

"I missed you," he whispered.

"Me, too." And standing there in his arms, his muscular thighs pressed against hers, she still missed him. Pushed up against each other wasn't close enough to touch the longing for whatever it was that they'd lost over the years.

His dark gaze met hers and her breath caught in her throat. She couldn't have looked away if she'd wanted to. His mouth hovered close to hers, a whisper of breath tickling her lips. He hesitated, and before she could think better of it, Nora closed the distance between them, standing on her tiptoes so that her lips met his. He took it from there, dipping his head down and sliding a hand through her hair. His other hand pressed against the small of her back, nudging her closer, closer against his muscular body, her bare legs against his jeans, her hands clutching the sides of his shirt. His lips moved over hers, confident and hungry, and when he finally pulled back, she was left weak-kneed and breathless.

"Been wanting to do that for a while," he said, running the pad of his thumb over her plumped lips.

She laughed softly. "Oh..."

"Don't worry," he said, his voice a husky growl. "We can chalk that up to an emotional evening, and tomorrow you won't have to think about it again."

Easton's gaze moved down to her lips again, then he smiled roguishly and took a step back, cool air rushing over her body. She didn't know what she thought, or what she wanted, but he wasn't asking for anything. He moved to the doorway and looked back.

"Good night," he said and then disappeared into the dark hallway.

Nora stood there, her fingers lightly touching her lips. He'd *kissed* her just now, and she realized that the attraction he felt for her was very, very mutual.

Nora went to close her bedroom door, and she paused, looking out into the hallway. All was quiet, except for the soft rustle of movement coming from the room next door. He was probably getting ready for bed, and she pulled her mind firmly away from that precipice.

If only she'd seen deeper into Easton's heart when they were younger…she might have been a bigger comfort to him, a better listener. If she'd realized then the man he'd mature into in a few years—but all of that was too late. If there was one thing the discovery of her father's unfaithfulness had taught her, it was that a man could be as loving and doting as her father had been, and he could still cheat, lie and hide his tracks. Nora needed to be able to count on a man for better or for worse, or those vows were pointless. She'd been lonely for what she and Easton had experienced together in that innocent adolescent friendship, but she'd been hungry for something more just now—something that hadn't existed before. She'd wanted security— she'd wanted kisses in the moonlight that didn't have to end, that could be hers and only hers…

Nora shut the door and slid back into her bed. Two and a half more hours until the girls needed another bottle. She'd best get some sleep.

Chapter Ten

The next afternoon Easton wrapped the starter in a clean rag then used another one to wipe the grease off his hands. He'd have Nora's truck up and running tonight as promised.

He'd left early that morning, not wanting to run into her after the kiss last night. He still carried that image of her in a knee-length nightgown—totally chaste by all accounts, but still... What was it about Nora that could make a granny nightgown alluring? If he hadn't left when he did, he wouldn't have stopped at holding her close, and he wouldn't have stopped at the kiss, either. Her bed had been right there—yeah, he'd noticed—and if he'd been listening to the thrum of the impulses surging through him, he would have nudged her over to those rumpled sheets and pulled her as close as two bodies could get.

Except he wasn't just a horny teenager; he was a grown man, and for the most part he didn't do stupid things he'd regret the next morning. He knew where this led—the same place it had led when they were teenagers. She was vulnerable right now, her life was upside down and she needed someone to lean on. His shoulders were broad enough for the weight of her burdens, and that was all she really wanted deep down—he was convinced of it. She'd been there for him, too, and he was grateful for that. But a moment of mutual comfort wouldn't turn into anything that would last. He knew better. He could try to convince himself that she was interested in a real relationship with him, but had she been, she'd have shown that interest long before now. When things got tough for Nora, she came to him. Then she left again. It was their pattern.

Easton didn't have the emotional strength right now to deal with yet another rejection from the one girl he'd always pined for. Pining didn't do a thing—even as a boy, longing for his mom to come home. Now she had, but it wasn't what he'd imagined. It hadn't smoothed things over—and it certainly wouldn't fix the past. He was a grown man now, and he wasn't willing to set himself up for more heartbreak. So he'd kissed Nora, and while he didn't regret it, he wasn't about to do it again. He'd been serious when he said he was chalking it up to an emotional night. He was letting them both off the hook.

He heard the scrape of boots on the cement floor, and Easton turned to see Dale Young, Cliff's brother-in-law. He was an older guy, skinny and tall with a prominent nose and gray brush of a mustache.

"Hey, Dale," Easton said. "What brings you here?"

He crossed the garage and shook the other man's hand.

"Just checking up on things," Dale said. "I told Dina

I'd come say howdy. One of your ranch hands told me where I could find you."

"Just getting a part for Nora's truck." Easton held it up. "So how've you been?"

"Not bad…" Dale winced. "The gossip around this place has been something fierce. My wife has been taking it personal."

Easton shrugged his assent to that. Nora and Dina were taking it hard, too.

"Did you know about the other woman?" Dale asked.

"Before my time," Easton said. "And from what I gather, it wasn't a lengthy affair. Just a mistake."

"Hmm." Dale grunted.

"I don't like how people are talking," Easton admitted. "Cliff was a good man—a solid neighbor, a helping hand. How many times did he help with a cattle drive or with hay baling when someone was sick?"

"Preaching to the choir," Dale replied. "I know you two were close. He was good to you, too."

The two men walked out of the garage into the sunlight, and Easton adjusted his hat to shade his eyes. Cliff had been good to him, and it wasn't just about the three acres and the old house. That land came complicated, and it had been rubbing at his conscience ever since Nora's return.

"Dale, I was wondering about that," Easton said, pausing. "The land he gave me, that is."

"Yeah?"

"It's your wife's grandparents' house," Easton said. "Does that rankle her at all, me having it? I'm not family."

Dale sucked in a deep breath then let it out slowly and shrugged. "A little, truthfully."

Easton expected as much.

"She'd never say nothing about it," Dale went on. "Cliff owned that house, and could do what he wanted with it. None of us expected that he'd just give it away like that, though."

"And you?" Easton pressed. "Do you have an issue with me living there?"

"Nah." Dale smoothed his fingers over his mustache. "It's a house, and Cliff wasn't a man to do something like that lightly. He gave it to you for a reason. He wanted you to have it."

A reason—that was what Easton needed to nail down. Why had Cliff done that—written over a piece of his family history?

"Before he died, he wanted me to move into that house and live there. He said he wanted someone to take care of the place for him. Thing is, I can't rest easy knowing that I'm sitting on land that means this much to the Carpenters. I mean, it's a godsend for me, but that's because I come from a hard place. I was just a cowboy who respected his boss. Nothing more and nothing less. Was I really worth that kind of gift? If I knew what made him do it, it might make it easier to carry on as he intended."

Because if Cliff had only been trying to keep him as an employee, he'd feel really bad about that. He didn't need to be bought off, especially with something that meant so much to the rest of the family. Now that Cliff was gone, Dina might be okay with replacing him eventually.

Dale nodded slowly. "I think Cliff had a big heart."

Was that it? Was this emotional?

"What do you mean by that?" Easton pressed.

"Meaning you weren't just an employee to him. He cared for you—and while you think you weren't family to him, there's three acres of land that begs to differ." Dale shrugged. "You mattered to him, and he made sure you were taken care of. God knows your own dad wasn't going to leave you nothing. People are gonna talk—and that's not gonna change. They'll talk about Cliff's affair, and about your land... It's what people do. If you really can't rest easy there, then sell it to Nora. You'd have some money to start fresh somewhere else, and she'd have that precious house back."

Nora's problem seemed to be that she had nowhere to call home in Hope anymore—nowhere truly hers. If she had that house back, the seat of her family's memories, then maybe she could have what she wanted most. And a fresh start for him...it gave him a little hopeful rush to even consider it right now.

"It's a good idea," Easton said with a nod. "Thanks."

"Not a problem." Dale eyed Easton for a moment. "Or marry her. That could take care of the family issue pretty quick."

Easton smiled wryly. "I've known Nora for a long time, Dale. I've been friend-zoned since we were fourteen."

Dale barked out a laugh and shook his head. "Those Carpenter women are a handful."

And Dale would know—he'd been married to Cliff Carpenter's sister for the last thirty-five years. But he had a point. Selling the house to Nora would take care of things right quick. She'd get the house she loved; he'd get a new start somewhere else. And if his mom could have a fresh start—all clean and respectable— then why not him? She'd left him behind in that hole with his father, but that didn't mean he had to stay here in Hope. What was holding him here now, after all? Cliff had passed on, his father had never had much right to Easton's loyalty and his mother was raising another son with her electrician husband, *Tom*.

This was a big country—heck even the state of Montana was pretty large. He'd had some job offers before; he'd be able to find another position without too much trouble—a new life where no one knew the skeletons in his closet. Everyone had issues—that wasn't the problem. It was having everyone know you well enough to be able to point out your issues plain as day. That was the aggravating part. But a chance at a life where no one else knew the things that stabbed him deepest? Well, that was a whole new kind of freedom that he longed to taste.

But still—that took walking away, and just leaving Nora and the babies. While it would solve everything, it would be hard. He wasn't a part of that family—wasn't that what he'd been acknowledging all along, that he wasn't really family? But still, while he may want a fresh start, a small and stupid part of him stayed the hopeful teenager, and saw Nora by his side.

His phone blipped and he looked down to see a text from his mom.

Hi Easton—how about Saturday at 11 at Beauty's Ice Cream? Brandon wants to meet you.

He stood, frozen for a moment, his mind spinning. She'd done it. She'd gotten that fresh start, and the thing he hated most about it was how blasted happy she looked now. A husband, another kid, a comfortable life... If his mom could do it, then why not him?

He texted back:

Sure. See you then.

Nora, Dina and Aunt Audrey sat around the kitchen table in the main house, mugs of coffee in front of them. Dale had left after lunch to go take a look at the ranch. With Cliff gone, Dale had taken it upon himself to make sure things didn't slump while Dina grappled with her grief. People could get taken advantage of during times of tragedy, and it took a family pulling together to make sure that didn't happen.

Lunch dishes were piled on the countertop, mugs of coffee replaced them on the scratched table and the women sat together, sipping their coffee, waiting for Dale to get back. Audrey bore a striking resemblance to her late brother. She had his mix of blond and white hair, the same stalky build, the same short fingers.

Audrey held sleeping Bobbie in her arms. Nora was snuggling Riley, and Rosie lay in her car seat. Dina's arms were empty. She leaned her elbows on the table, a half-finished mug of coffee in front of her.

"They look like Carpenters," Audrey said. "I can see it in the shape of their faces. All the Carpenter babies have these little chins."

Dina glanced at Audrey, her expression blank.

"They're here now," Audrey said pointedly. "You might want to accept it, Dina."

"And if Dale had another family somewhere?" Dina retorted. "You'd just open your arms to all of his grandchildren?"

Audrey smoothed a hand over Bobbie's downy head. "Dale isn't the type—"

"And Cliff was?" Dina demanded. "You're telling me you saw that coming?"

"I told myself I wouldn't mention it, but is it possible that you were a tad too controlling with Cliff?" Audrey's voice stayed quiet, but her tone hardened. "He had to come home and ask you before he did *anything*. Maybe he had a small revolt—an inappropriate one, obviously, but—" She paused and put her attention back into the baby.

Dina's eyes flashed, but her chin quivered with repressed tears. She pushed her mug away and stood up, turning her back on them and stalking toward the kitchen window.

"What do you know about my parents' marriage?" Nora snapped.

"He was my brother," Audrey replied. "I knew *him*."

"Dad wasn't whipped," Nora retorted. "He respected her opinion. And what did he come home and discuss with her—lending you and Dale money? Has it ever occurred to you that he wanted to say no to giving you more cash, and needed some distance to do it?"

The room hummed with tension, and Nora looked at her mother's rigid back. This was what Dina was facing now—judgment from women who didn't want to believe it could just as easily have happened to them. Dina would be the one to blame, because if it was her fault, then the others could avoid her fate. Heaven knew no one would want to cheat on a woman like Audrey—always so virtuous and right all the time. Nora suppressed the urge to roll her eyes.

"All I'm trying to say," Audrey said at last, "is that these children are here, and they are my relatives, too. If you can't be a granny to them, Dina, then I'll step in."

Was that a solution? Audrey was a blood relative to these baby girls, and if she'd be "Grandma," then perhaps it would let her own mother off the hook. Audrey lovingly stroked Bobbie's hand with one finger, but Nora caught the look of stricken grief on her mother's face as she turned back to face them.

Dina would be pushed out. Nora could see how this would unfold. The girls would be loved and spoiled by Audrey and Dale, but that wouldn't stop gossip about their grandfather, and it would only put Dina, the loving wife of their grandfather, on the sidelines where she would still be blamed for her husband's cheating. Because if there was one thing about Audrey, it was her utter conviction that she was right.

Nora didn't want Dina to be Grandma because of

her relationship to Cliff; she'd wanted Dina because of her relationship to *her*. Audrey's offer wasn't a solution so much as a threat—step up as grandparent, or live forever in the shadows.

Dale's boots echoed on the side steps, and the door opened. He took off his hat as he came in.

"Howdy," he said, then he stopped short. "Everything okay in here?"

"Just snuggling babies," Audrey said, a shade too chipper. "Why don't you come hold this little angel, Dale?"

Dale's gaze moved to Dina then back to his wife. He seemed to do the math pretty quickly, because his mustache twitched a couple of times, then he said, "We'd better get back, Aud."

"Seriously, Dale, come and see these little treasures…" Audrey leaned down and breathed in next to Bobbie's head. "They smell so good."

"Aud." He didn't say anything else—his tone was enough, and he stared at his wife flatly until she sighed, rose to her feet and brought Bobbie over to Nora.

"You remember what I said, Nora," she said quietly. "There's more than one way to be family."

Dale waited by the door until Audrey had collected her purse and said her goodbyes. Before shutting the door, Dale cast Nora an apologetic look.

"Take care now, Nora," he said with that usual flat tone of his. "And take care of your mom, too, okay?"

"Bye, Uncle Dale." She smiled, but she wasn't sure she pulled it off.

Then they were gone.

Nora sat with her mother in silence. The two babies slept on in Nora's arms and she looked at their peaceful faces. The clock ticked audibly from the wall, and Nora felt like her heart was filled with water. This was a mess. Audrey would make her mother miserable for the rest of her life if she was given the chance. Dina and Audrey had respected each other, but there had always been a little bit of a chilly distance there—history that Nora didn't know about, no doubt.

"Was I controlling?" Dina asked hollowly.

"Not with Dad," Nora said. "You were the toughie with me, though."

"I was the toughie because your dad wouldn't discipline you," Dina said with a sigh. "He wanted to be the good guy all the time, so he'd leave getting you back into line for me. Do you know how badly I wanted to be the good guy every once in a while?"

"Really?" Perhaps their marriage had been more complicated than Nora realized. She blinked back sudden tears. Her dad had been the quiet strength in her life, the one who would nod slowly and say, "Your mother isn't as wrong as you think…" But still, someone had to draw lines and give lectures. Just not Cliff.

"Dad just did things differently." That was probably an understatement. They were only finding out now how differently he'd been doing things.

"Yeah." Dina rubbed a hand over her eyes.

Nora hadn't told her mother about the letters Easton had found yet—she hadn't been sure it was a good idea, but now she reconsidered. Audrey would love nothing more than to pass around that Cliff had been keeping up a long-term romance with Angela, but that wasn't the case.

"Easton found some letters that Angela wrote to Dad," Nora said. "They didn't seem to have any kind of ongoing affair. But she kept Dad up-to-date on Mia, it seems."

Dina frowned. "What—did he have a secret post office box or something?"

"Yes."

Dina shook her head but didn't say anything. Another betrayal. Another secret. How many would they unearth before this was over?

"Mia really hated him as a kid," Nora said. "She wrote him a letter telling him how much she hated him for not being a part of her life."

"I hate him right now, too," Dina said, and a tear escaped and trickled down her cheek. She wiped it away then sucked in a breath, visibly rallying herself again. "It's just as well we've canceled the corn roast."

"Is that what you really want?" Nora asked.

"What I want is to have my husband back," Dina retorted. "And for his sister to go jump in a lake."

"Yeah, she's not my favorite, either."

Nora looked out the kitchen window, her mind going back over all those other Carpenter corn roasts—the fun times, the laughter… Her dad had always been the center of it all, barbecuing up burgers for everyone. They could abandon the tradition, or they could face it.

"Will it help to skip it?" Nora asked after a moment. "I mean—they'll talk anyway, but if we call off the corn roast and keep to ourselves, will they talk more?"

"That corn roast turned into tradition over the years," Dina said thoughtfully. "What if... I mean, it might be our last one, but I think you're right. Let them come and see us in our complicated mess. The less they see of us, the more they'll talk. And with any luck at all, Audrey will get food poisoning."

Nora barked out a laugh. "Okay. Sure. In Dad's honor."

Rosie started to fuss from her car seat, squirming and letting out a whine. She hated being out of arms, that little girl, but Nora had both Riley and Bobbie in her arms and she couldn't pick up a third. Nora glanced pleadingly at her mother. "Help me?"

Dina slowly undid the buckles and lifted Rosie into her arms. She stood there, looking down into the baby's tiny face, her expression softening.

"They do look like Carpenters," she said. "Your idiot father would have been so proud..."

Nora felt laughter bubbling up inside her. "Are you going to call him my idiot father for the rest of your life?"

"Yes." Dina smiled wryly. "I think I will. He's certainly earned it."

Rosie immediately settled now that she was in Dina's arms, letting out a soft sigh of contentment. It was impossible not to fall for these babies, and Nora could see that reality in her mother's face as she gently patted the diapered rump.

"You were this small once," Dina said. "And it was easier then. So much less complicated."

"Are you saying it'll only get worse—this mess, I mean—as the girls get older?"

Dina nodded slowly. "I'm afraid that's the case, but I can't make those calls for you, Nora. You're a grown woman now, and these are your choices."

They were her choices, but some choices had very little wiggle room.

"I've been looking into adoption for the girls," Nora said. "Another family, I mean. It's all so messed up here, and I can't do this without you. I'm certainly not doing it with Audrey as my go-to support, either."

Her mother met her gaze sadly. "You'd give them up?"

"I don't think this situation is good for them," Nora said. "We could hope that things would get easier, but what if they don't?"

Dina didn't answer. Nora knew that her mother couldn't help her to make this choice. She was the only one who could decide what she could live with. Easton's mother had left him, and he resented her so much because she hadn't been thinking about Easton and what was best for him—she'd only been thinking of her own escape. Nora didn't want to make that mistake. She needed to do what was best for the girls, regardless of what it did to her.

"I emailed an adoption agent," Nora went on. "We went back and forth a little bit, and she'll come by and see us next week, give us some more information."

She tried to blink back the tears that welled up in her eyes, but they slipped down her cheeks. She hated this—she loved these girls so much that she was willing to give them up. But it hurt so much more than she'd thought it would. Dina came over to Nora, and Nora leaned her face into her mother's side. She could feel her mother's fingers smoothing over the top of her head, just like when she was little.

"I'm so sorry, baby," Dina whispered. "I'm so, so sorry…"

They both were—everyone was. It seemed that pain was the price paid for having loved.

Chapter Eleven

Saturday morning Easton pulled up in front of Beauty's Ice Cream. His mom had brought him here once that he could recall—after some massive fight she and Dad had had, and she'd bought him an ice cream cone and stared at him morosely while he ate it. Treats didn't come often, so he'd scarfed it down, but he could still remember offering her a bite. She'd said no. Funny the things that stuck.

He parked next to the red SUV—she was here already, apparently. Glancing in her window, he saw a kid's hoodie in the backseat, next to an empty chip bag. This was it. He was about to meet his brother for the first time, and he honestly couldn't say he was looking forward to it.

Beauty's Ice Cream was a quaint little shop with a red and white awning. Windows lined the front, and he could see the back of a woman's head in a booth. Was that Mom? He assumed so. Most guys could pinpoint the backs of their own mothers' heads easily, but his mom had changed a lot over the last twenty years.

Mom... He still felt a well of emotion at the thought

of her, and he hated that. It would be easier to just be angry, or to resent her, but his true feelings were more complicated—so much more difficult to separate.

He opened the front door and entered the air-conditioned interior. Trent, the owner, stood behind the counter. He wore a heavy metal shirt, partially covered by a white apron, and he gave Easton a nod.

"Morning," Trent said. "What can I get for you?"

"Uh—" Easton glanced toward his mom, his gaze landing on the sandy-haired boy. He had a sundae in front of him, chocolate sauce in the corners of his mouth, and Easton found all of his thoughts suddenly drain from his head. "Nothing right now," he said, then angled over to the booth.

"Easton." His mother smiled up at him then scooted over. "Come sit."

Brandon stared at Easton wide-eyed then took a bite of ice cream as if on autopilot. Easton scooted into the semicircular booth so that his mom sat at the bottom of the curve between both sons.

"Brandon, this is your brother," she said.

"Hey," Easton said. "Nice to meet you."

"He's a *man*," Brandon whispered, eyeing his mother questioningly.

"Yes. He's grown-up."

Brandon's clothes looked new, and he had an iPad on the table next to him, a set of headphones draped around his neck. The kid had stuff to entertain him, that was for sure. Easton had never had a Game Boy or decent headphones. His headphones had always been taped together where they broke so that they wouldn't fit right.

They were silent for a few beats, and Easton searched his mind for something to say.

"Easton is a ranch manager," his mother said at last. "He runs someone's ranch for them—he's very good."

"Oh." Brandon frowned slightly. "I'm in grade three."

"Yeah…" Could this get any more awkward? This kid didn't care about meeting his mom's adult son. If anything, Easton's existence was confusing.

"Brandon loves horses," his mother tried again. "He draws them all the time."

"Not anymore," Brandon replied. "I draw monster trucks now."

Easton wondered if this had been a mistake. What had his mother been expecting from this little get-together— warmth and coziness? She hadn't provided that when she'd been in his life, and it wasn't going to suddenly materialize because they all shared some DNA.

"Mom brought me here once when I was your age," Easton said.

Brandon looked around. "Here?"

"Yeah. She used to live in this town with me and my dad."

"She lives in Billings now," Brandon said, and Easton caught the flicker of fear in the boy's eyes. He was eight years old, and he was scared of losing his mom. That was something Easton could sympathize with. Eight was too young to worry about those things, and this kid had all the security that Easton had lacked growing up. He had the clothes, the toys, the stay-at-home mom who drove him to chess practice.

"I know," Easton said quietly. "I'm grown-up, so I don't need our mom to take care of me anymore. She belongs with you. So don't worry about me trying to keep her here."

His mother's eyes filled with tears, and she put a hand out, tentatively touching Easton's arm. What, did she suddenly want to be needed in his life?

"Dad was right about me being okay," Easton said, turning to his mom.

"I'm glad," she said. "I'd hoped so… I made mistakes, son. I wasn't sure if I'd want to do this in front of Brandon, but I think it's better for him to see his mother acknowledge her mistakes than to wonder about them for the rest of his life."

"Were you a little kid when Mom left?" Brandon asked.

"Yeah." The same age as Brandon, but he wouldn't torment the boy with that. "I was. I had my dad, but he drank a lot, so…" He sucked in a breath. He didn't exactly want to horrify the boy. "You know, I got a job, and my boss was a really decent guy. He helped me figure things out, and he taught me how to work a ranch. So I was okay, actually."

"Didn't you miss her?" The kid was connecting the dots here. He was thinking about what it would be like to face his young existence without his mom by his side.

"I did," Easton nodded, a lump rising in his throat. "I missed her a whole lot."

Mom reached out and brushed Brandon's hair off his forehead, and Easton saw it—his fantasy of a loving mother being played out in the life of his half brother. He'd longed for a hand to brush his hair off his forehead just like that...

Easton cleared his throat. "So tell me about your dad."

"Dad works a lot," Brandon said. "But when he's home, he plays LEGO with me. I've got the whole cops and robbers setup, and I play cops and Dad plays robbers. Have you seen the new prison?"

Brandon scooped up his iPad and turned it on. "I'll find it for you—Mom, is there Wi-Fi here?"

For the next few minutes they talked about Brandon's love of LEGO, they discovered that Beauty's Ice Cream did not, in fact, have Wi-Fi and Easton ordered himself a chocolate cone. Brandon was a sweet kid—an untarnished version of himself at that age. Easton had grown up with substance abuse, poverty, neglect, and he'd raised himself. He'd been tougher than other kids his age, and while he used to think of himself as resilient, he wondered now if he'd merely been damaged.

Brandon was smart, intuitive, passionate about his interests. But he wasn't tough—his emotions swam over his face and he didn't hide behind a mask of indifference. Easton was willing to bet that this kid didn't know half the curse words he did at that age. Maybe this was what he'd have been like if he'd been raised in a safer environment.

"Do you have a girlfriend?" Brandon asked him.

"No—" Easton paused and looked into the face of

this boy who was finally relaxing a little bit. His little brother. Whatever happened all those years ago, this kid was related to him, and he'd probably want to be in his life somewhat as the years went on. He could close off and keep this impersonal, or he could share something. He decided on the latter.

"There's a woman I care about a lot," Easton said.

"Who is she?" Brandon asked.

"Her name is Nora, and I've had a crush on her since I was a bit older than you. Do you like girls yet?"

Brandon shook his head. "But they like me. Isabel T. said that Olivia liked me last year. I think she did. She was really annoying."

So it began. Easton shot his mother a rueful smile.

"Does Nora like you back?" Brandon asked. "Because if she likes you back, then she's your girlfriend."

"It's a little more complicated when you get older," Easton said.

Life was pretty simple if you were a kid—especially a protected kid like Brandon. But life had a way of getting difficult when you least expected it; of kicking your expectations out from under you. Easton needed a woman who would face the hard times with him, be the shoulder he needed once in a while. Love wasn't enough to make a relationship last, and Easton had been let down in life too many times to take a risk when it came to a life partner. And Nora was a risk. A beautiful, passionate, intoxicating risk. She could be there for him when he needed some emotional support— like that kiss in her bedroom in the moonlight—but Nora also had a pattern of taking off again once her own problems were solved. Had she changed now that she had the babies to care for? Or was he just hoping?

An image rose in his mind of that morning he'd woken up to find his mother gone. His father was drinking already at the kitchen table, and he'd pointed to the note on the fridge.

"Your mom took off," his father said, words slightly slurred.

"What?" Easton hadn't believed it. She wouldn't just leave *him*. He was her kid, and moms didn't walk out on their kids. He'd searched around, looking for the things that cemented her in their home—her nightgown, her jewelry, the hairbrush that always had hair stuck in it like a small animal. They were gone. Her clothes—the nicer ones—were gone, too. There was an empty space in his parents' closet. Her purse—that sagging bag he was forbidden to touch—was gone from its place on the back of a kitchen chair.

He could still remember what it felt like as the truth dawned on him—Mom was gone. He'd headed up to his room and sobbed his heart out. He wasn't safe alone with Dad—he knew that well enough. He'd have to fend for himself now, because his father sure wouldn't be doing his laundry or cooking him meals. Dad didn't make school lunches.

And when he crawled into his bed that night, the house silent except for the sound of the TV downstairs, he'd closed his eyes and imagined that his mother was stroking his hair away from his face...

"Will you come visit us?" Brandon asked, and Easton pushed the memories back.

His mother looked at him, her brow furrowed, and she clutched at the handle of a new purse—something expensive by the look of it.

"We would really like that," his mom said. "Tom wants to meet you, too. You'll like him, I think."

Had she ever wondered how he went to sleep at night without her there to say good-night? Or if he was eating properly, or if he was embarrassed at school because his dad had drunk away the money for bigger clothes? Did she ever wonder if she'd broken his heart beyond repair?

"Okay. Sure. One of these days."

His mom was back. As weird as this felt. She looked so successful now, so put together. Her hair was nicely done, her makeup making her look a little younger. And he was glad that she was doing it right with her second-born. That was something, wasn't it?

Even if it had all started with an escape…from him.

THAT EVENING NORA sat on the front steps of the homestead, her arms wrapped around her knees. She'd found an old framed photo up in the bedroom closet, and she sat outside in the lowering light, looking at it. She hadn't seen this one before. There were a certain number of photos that everyone had a copy of—her great-grandparents' wedding portrait, a picture at some family member's funeral with all the extended family present, grouped around the coffin. There were a few others of her great-grandparents and their children seated on kitchen chairs stuck out in the yard—their equivalent of a family portrait. But this photo was different than the others.

The photo was a small rectangle, not even filling up the entire frame. It depicted her great-grandparents standing alone, likely in their first years of marriage because there were no children about. They were in front of a large tractor—the kind that would be in a museum these days. Her great-grandmother was wearing a pair of overalls, her light hair swept back by the wind, and she leaned against a tractor tire. Her great-grandfather was in a pair of patched jeans, looking at his young wife with adoration. His shirt was open a few buttons, and his sleeves were rolled up to reveal tanned forearms. It was such a perfect moment, and Nora could understand why someone had framed it.

Tomorrow they'd have the corn roast, and somehow she thought her great-grandmother might have made the same choice she and Dina had, to face it head-on. There was something brave and almost defiant in her eyes, and when Nora looked closer at the photo, she noticed something she hadn't seen before in the other, more formal pictures.

Mia looked an awful lot like their great-grandmother. Wow. Funny how DNA worked. Nora didn't take after their great-grandmother physically. She looked more like her mother's side of the family, but she'd still felt a great connection to the Carpenter lineage. Yet Mia, who was the accidental love child conceived during some tryst, was the spitting image of their ancestor. Genetics certainly didn't take legitimacy into account. Mia would have liked to know this, Nora realized sadly. She might have even taken some pride in knowing where her looks came from.

Easton's rusty truck rumbled up the drive, and she watched as he parked and got out. He slammed the door behind him and came toward her. He paused before he reached her then took off his hat.

"Hey," he said. "Care for some company?"

"Sure." She moved over and he sat down next to her, tossing his hat onto the step beside them. His hair was disheveled, an errant piece of hay stuck into one of his flattered curls. He was dusty, and he smelled like hard work and sunshine.

"How was your day?" she asked.

"Not bad." He nodded slowly. "I met my half brother."

"Really?" She shot him a look of surprise. "What's he like?"

"A nice kid," he said. "He's got the whole package— parents who love each other, financial security, all the attention that he needs."

"That's a good thing," she said. "Right?"

"Yup." He smiled wanly. "At least Mom figured it all out eventually."

"Will you see them again?" she asked.

"Probably," he said. "But I'm not ready to hammer out Christmas plans or anything. I'm taking it slow."

That was fair. Still, she could see how much this had hurt him. Sometimes when a person's deepest longing was fulfilled, it hurt as much as it healed. Mia might have discovered the same thing if she'd ever met their father. To Nora, her dad was a superhero. To Mia, he was the selfish jerk who missed her childhood. It might have hurt a lot to see the parenting he was capable of.

Easton nodded toward the photo in her hands. "What's that?"

"My great-grandparents," she said. "I found it up in the closet in your guest bedroom."

He leaned closer to look, slipping a hand behind her as he did so, but it didn't seem intentional. Without really thinking about it, she leaned back against his arm. He looked startled, then he nodded back to the photo.

"He loves her," Easton said, his voice low and next to her ear.

"They were the great Carpenter love story," she said. Easton straightened, pulled away. She swallowed, trying not to let her discomfiture show. "She came from a moderately wealthy family in the city. She and my great-grandpa met at a dance, I think. I don't know how that worked out exactly, but she ended up eloping with him. It took years for her family to forgive her. Even then, she never got a penny from them."

Easton smiled then shrugged. "I'd say she made the right choice."

"They ended up having seven children together," Nora said. "But that picture—I've never seen it before."

"No?"

He leaned forward, his elbows on his knees, and she found herself so tempted to slip her arm through the gap and take his hand. Why was her mind constantly going there with him?

"It makes you wonder," she said quietly, "if he was faithful."

"Why wouldn't he be?" Easton asked. "He had a beautiful wife."

"So did my father."

That was the problem all along—there had been no good reason for her father's cheating. Not that there ever was when someone did that kind of thing. Had he loved Angela? Had it been meaningless sex, or had he fallen for her on some level? And if it was love, how could he claim to love his wife at the same time? She'd believed that her father was above that kind of ugliness, but she'd seen that he wasn't.

"I saw my aunt today," she said after a moment of silence. "She blamed Mom for Dad's affair."

"What?" Easton straightened and shot her an incredulous look. "How'd she figure?"

"She said Mom was too bossy and she implied that it was understandable that Dad would use cheating as a way to gain a bit of freedom from her."

"That's BS."

"Yeah, well... I always thought my parents had a marriage of steel. My dad would come and talk to my mom before he made any decision. I mean, *any* decision. He wouldn't buy a cow without her input, and it wasn't because she demanded it. He just really wanted to know what she thought first. But Audrey said that Mom was too controlling. Was I wrong about it? Did I see a strong marriage, where really my father was suffocating?"

Easton was silent—probably the smart choice, she realized wryly. He wouldn't know any more about their marriage than she did.

"Because I'm just like my mom in a lot of ways, Easton."

That was what scared her. She and her mother were both strong personalities with their own way of doing things. So if Dina wasn't woman enough to deserve fidelity…if Nora's mother was too controlling or too opinionated…if there was something innately unworthy about Dina that made Cliff feel like cheating was an option for him…what about Nora?

"Your dad talked about your mom a lot," Easton said. "He said he was lucky to have her. He said he wouldn't have been half as successful without her, so his advice to me was to find a good woman with a head on her shoulders and get married. He said two were better than one. I saw your mom consulting with your dad just as often. They relied on each other. He loved her… I don't know what happened when he cheated, but I do know that he loved her."

"And yet, he did cheat." She'd never make her peace with this. How could someone claim to love a woman and then step out on her? How could he see how much she added to his life and then betray her?

"Maybe he lived to regret it," Easton said. "Sometimes that's all you've got to hang your hat on—that the person who wronged you regretted it."

"Did your mom regret leaving you like she did?" Nora asked.

"I think so," he said.

"And is that enough for you?" She arched an eyebrow and caught his gaze.

"No," he admitted. "But it's a start."

"They were no better than we are…just the generation before us. So what makes us so different? We have their DNA, we come from the same genetic line and our formative years were under their care."

Easton reached over and moved a hair out of her eyes. His fingers lingered against her cheek, and those dark eyes met hers tenderly. He didn't seem to have an answer for her, but he leaned in and kissed her lips gently. He pulled back then moved in again, sliding an arm around her and slipping a hand across her thigh as his warm lips met hers.

From the open window above, a baby's cry filtered down to them. Nora pulled back, heat rising in her cheeks. Why did she keep falling into kissing this man? She swallowed hard and rose to her feet. She was supposed to know better, and the minute her pulse slowed down, she'd remember why.

"I'd better go see what the trouble is," she said and headed into the house.

Chapter Twelve

The next morning was Sunday, the day of the corn roast, and Nora's cell phone rang while she was feeding Bobbie. She fumbled with the phone and picked it up, pinching the handset between her shoulder and ear. Bobbie's big brown eyes were fixed on Nora's face as she drank.

"Hello?"

"Hi, is this Nora Carpenter?"

"Speaking." A dribble of milk dripped down Bobbie's chin, disappearing into the cloth Nora had waiting on the baby's chest. She was getting better at this—anticipating burps and dribbles like a pro.

"This is Tina Finlayson from the adoption agency. Do you have time to talk?"

After a few brief pleasantries, Tina got down to business. "I've just had a home visit with some new clients this morning, and I have a feeling this is something that would interest you."

Nora looked at the clock on the wall. It was nine in the morning on a weekend. "That's early."

"They have a toddler who is an early riser. In my line of work, I make a point of being flexible."

She felt a wave of regret. Emails were one thing, but a phone call made all of this feel a lot more real. Was she absolutely certain about this?

"I haven't made my decision yet about whether I'll be finding another home for them," Nora qualified. "I know we've been emailing—"

"I don't mean for this to pressure you, but it might help to have some concrete information to work with. Are you interested in knowing a bit about them?"

Nora adjusted Bobbie in her arms, and the infant stretched out a leg. This wasn't a decision—it was only getting some facts. Right? That was what she'd been telling herself all along.

"All right," she agreed.

"These are people in a suburb of Billings," Tina went on. "He's a children's psychologist and she's a stay-at-home mom. They live in a large home, are financially secure and they're looking to expand their family. They have one adopted son who is three right now, and they are looking to adopt siblings. They'd love newborns, but they know that isn't always possible."

Nora realized she'd been holding her breath and she released it. They sounded perfect, actually.

"Would they be able to deal with triplets?" she asked.

"The mother has two sisters living in the same neighborhood," Tina went on. "And his parents live on a nearby acreage where they have horses and a hobby farm. So they'd have plenty of support in baby care."

A family that could offer the girls everything from cousins and grandparents to horseback riding on weekends. A father who was trained in child psychology would be an excellent support as they grew up, and a mom at home with them, too. They'd even have an older brother to grow up with.

What could Nora offer? She had a job in Billings—so she couldn't stay home with them. There would be day care, a single mom struggling to make ends meet and little extended family if Nora wanted to protect the girls from all the talk. But they would be loved. The most valuable thing she could offer was her heart, and right now that hardly seemed enough.

"Do they know about the girls?" Nora asked.

"I told them only the basics," Tina said. "That you weren't positive about what you wanted to do yet, but there was the possibility of three newborns becoming available. They were very eager to hear about them."

Of course. For another family, these three babies would be an answered prayer, a dream come true. Didn't the girls deserve to be wanted that desperately?

"Maybe I could meet them," Nora said.

"That would be wonderful," Tina agreed. "Don't feel pressured, but we could set up a little meeting where you could see them in person, get a feel for the type of family they are and you could see where you stand then. They might even be willing to have an open adoption where you could receive updates on how the girls are doing and perhaps be included in some major life events."

Not a complete goodbye…that might be something.

Nora's parental leave wouldn't last forever, and right now she was getting a fraction of her normal pay. Maybe it was better to meet this family before she got so attached to the triplets that she couldn't possibly change her mind.

"Are they free today?" she asked.

"Let me call them and see if we can set something up. I'm sure they'd be very happy to meet with you."

As it turned out, the family was more than happy to meet with her that day. Dina agreed to watch the babies, and Nora drove the three hours into Billings. Her GPS led her down the wide streets of a new subdivision, large houses on either side of the road. It was picturesque, idyllic city life. This was the kind of neighborhood that Nora couldn't hope to afford.

She found the house, and when she parked in the driveway, the front door opened and the dad came out, a toddler in his arms.

"Hi," he said, holding out his hand to shake hers as she slammed the driver's side door shut behind her. "I'm Mike. This here is Bryce."

Nora shook his hand then smiled at the toddler. He was clean with blond curls and new clothes.

"Nice to meet you both," she said. "I didn't bring the girls—my mom is watching them right now." Why did she feel the need to explain to these people?

"Totally understandable," Mike said and as she came around the truck she saw his wife, Sarah. She was pretty—brunette waves framing her face, big eyes and plump lips. She looked like she'd give good hugs. Blast it—why did she have to be so perfect?

But this wasn't a competition. This was about a situation beyond her control, and what would be better for the girls. Yet somehow, Nora didn't much like this motherly looking woman. They shook hands, too.

Tina had arrived before Nora had, so they had some professional guidance for their meeting. And over the course of the next hour, Nora toured their home, which had two extra bedrooms that weren't being used, a hot tub out back and a large vegetable garden that Sarah apparently had time to keep up. The kitchen was covered in little drawings that Bryce had done—scratching on paper with a fisted crayon, by the looks of it.

The house was clean, and the couple was affectionate and seemed to be in a secure and happy marriage. They even showed her some family photo albums from their wedding onward. They seemed to travel a lot.

"What are you looking for in a family for the girls?" Sarah asked once they were all seated in the living room. Nora had an untouched iced tea in front of her. Tina was smiling encouragingly at all of them.

"I don't know exactly," Nora said. Was there anything this family was missing? "A loving home, enough money to raise them well, a supportive extended family…"

Sarah and Mike exchanged a hopeful smile.

"Do you have any questions for us?" Mike asked.

"Have you considered an open adoption?" Nora asked. "It's going to be so hard to let go of them, and…" She didn't even know how to finish that.

"I had mentioned that it was a possibility," Tina said, her tone professional.

"We'd be willing to talk about that," Mike said with a nod. "They used to think that just closing all those doors was best for the children, but not anymore. It's good for kids to know that it was hard for their families to give them up. And if they can have contact with their birth family—limited, of course, without drama and stress—it's thought to be better for the kids overall."

"And we're interested in what's best for the children," Sarah added. "Children aren't owned, they're lent to us by God. And that's not an honor we take lightly."

"How much contact with the girls would you want?" Mike asked, and Nora didn't miss the caution that entered his tone.

"I don't even know." Nora swallowed then heaved a sigh. She felt like she was failing here—sitting in the living room of a "better" family, interviewing a couple that would be a stronger support to the babies she adored.

"Do you have any pictures of them?" Sarah asked.

Nora shook her head, and she suddenly felt protective. She didn't want to share photos of the girls. She didn't want to get this couple's hopes up, either. Knowing that a couple was interested in adopting the babies was one thing, but seeing that interest shining in their eyes hit Nora in a whole new place. This was real—too real. But she was here to see who they were—what they had to offer.

"They're two weeks old now," Nora said. "Their names are Riley, Rosie and Roberta."

"My grandmother's name was Rosie," Sarah said with an encouraging smile.

Would they even get to keep their names? Or would Bobbie turn into a Tiffany or an Elsa? All things that Nora hadn't thought about until this moment. And she'd have no control over that. This couple could rename them, and who would Nora be to complain? This room was suddenly feeling very small, and Nora glanced toward the door.

"To be honest," Nora said, "I haven't made up my mind. I'm pretty sure Tina told you that."

"Yes, it was clear," Mike said. "We aren't trying to pressure you."

Of course not. They were trying to impress her, show her the beautiful home they could give to the girls, if only Nora could find it in her to walk away from them.

"I love these girls." Tears misted Nora's eyes. "If I could provide for them, I'd keep them in a heartbeat. I don't want to do this. At all. I hate this, as a matter of fact."

"We understand." Sarah leaned forward. "It can't be easy."

Why did this woman have to be sympathetic, too? Couldn't she just show a crack already? Reveal some imperfection?

Bryce sidled up to his mother and she scooped him into her arms. He settled into his mother's lap, and she smoothed his hair with one porcelain hand. One day in the not-too-distant future, the girls would be toddlers like Bryce, and they'd be coming for hugs and attention—reminders that they mattered. Did Nora want to give that up? Or did she want to be the one who got to scoop them into her lap and cuddle them close? Could she really let another woman do that?

This wasn't about what she wanted…this was about her financial and emotional reality. If she'd given birth to them herself, she might feel better about dragging them through hard times in her wake, but she wasn't their biological mother. And they deserved better than what she could offer.

She looked at her watch. It was only one-thirty, but it was a three-hour drive back, and they still had the corn roast today. She'd seen enough of this couple to know what they could offer, and it wasn't Mike and Sarah who were the problem.

"Thank you for meeting with me." Nora stood up abruptly. "I have a lot to think over."

Everyone else stood, too, and Nora looked around herself for a moment. She held all the power right now, and they were all being incredibly nice about it… What was the polite way to get out of here?

"If you'd like to talk further, Mike and Sarah, you can give me a call and I'll contact Nora on your behalf. And the same goes for you, Nora." Tina was handing out business cards. "Sometimes after everyone has had a chance to think things through, choices are a little easier. This has been a very good start."

Tina made it all sound so normal, but nothing about this felt normal. Mike and Sarah were a lovely couple, and she hoped they managed to adopt a whole heap of kids, because they had a lot to offer. But *her* girls…

Nora said her goodbyes—shook hands, thanked people for their time—and then escaped to her truck. She needed to call her mom and see how the babies were doing, and then she needed to get back. This was the longest she'd been away from the girls since their birth, and instead of a welcome break the way coffee with Kaitlyn had been, this felt like guilt-ridden abandonment.

Was it possible that she'd already passed the point of no return—that she was selfish enough to put her needs before what was best for the girls?

EASTON LOOKED FORWARD to the corn roast every year—light duties, good food and a chance to relax. This year was the first one without Cliff. In a way, today would be goodbye to the boss they'd all loved.

The day started out like any other with general ranching duties, but when those were complete, he and some other ranch hands started the fire pits that would be used to boil corn and bake potatoes. Several barbecues would cook up everything from sausages to steaks. Then they'd indulge in a veritable feast.

"Tony, carry that tub of ice over to the table," Easton said, and the ranch hand in question gave a nod and headed in that direction.

Trucks were arriving in a steady flow now—family giving hugs and waving to each other. Dale and Audrey arrived, and Dale spotted him across the yard and tapped his hat in a salute. Audrey made straight for the babies, but there were already a few ladies who'd beat her there.

He found himself watching the hubbub around the babies more closely than he needed to. Nora was there—she had it well in hand. He had no reason to supervise, but he made note of where the girls were. Audrey had Rosie, Nora held Bobbie and another aunt held Riley, but then there was a trade off and someone else had Bobbie—why on earth was he bothering about this?

Easton pulled his attention away and noticed Dina coming in his direction.

"Easton!" she called. "We need to bring one more table out to where the barbecues are—do you mind?"

"Yes, ma'am," he replied, touching the rim of his hat.

Easton gestured for another ranch hand to help him, and they headed around the side of the barn to the shed where folding tables and chairs were stored. They returned a few minutes later, carrying the large table between them, and that was when he spotted it…

Tony was moving a box of unshucked corn, and as he turned, he swung the box past a woman who had Riley in her arms. The box came within a breath of the baby. Easton's temper snapped and he dropped his end of the table and marched in Tony's direction.

"What was that?" he bellowed.

"What?" Tony looked around.

"Did you see her?" Easton demanded. "You came within an inch of the baby!"

"There was lots of space," Tony retorted. "It's fine."

"It's not fine," Easton said. "Get over here!"

Tony complied, and Easton couldn't quite explain

this level of rage. He normally operated on a "no harm, no foul" philosophy, but there was something about those babies that sparked a protective instinct in him.

"The corner of a box connecting with a baby's head would be fatal," Easton said, keeping his voice low and his glowering gaze firmly on the ranch hand in front of him. "There are three newborns and numerous kids around. You walk carefully and look where you're going."

Tony seemed annoyed, but he nodded anyway, and Easton let him get on with his work. Another ranch hand helped get the table over to the barbecues, and Easton looked around. It was all running smoothly. One of the large cauldrons of water had already come to a boil and two uncles were feeding corn into it. A couple of ranch hands were checking the temperature of the barbecues. The food was starting, the setup was virtually complete and now they'd all cook and eat. Mission accomplished. He still felt irritable and unsettled. What was his problem?

Nora stood with a group of family. Kaitlyn was there, too—and across the yard her husband, Brody, was chatting with some other men. But it wasn't Kaitlyn who drew his eye—it never had been. Nora's hair shone golden in the smattering of sunlight, and his heart sped up a little at the sight of her. His irritation wasn't rational. Nora was being friendly, but there was still a gulf between them—family and staff were in different ranks around here. And he wanted more. Blast it, that was the problem—he'd been happy enough over on this side of things when Cliff was around. He'd been grateful for the opportunity to work here, grateful for a boss who was willing to help him mature as a rancher. But now it wasn't that he wasn't grateful... he wasn't satisfied.

Easton was respected, liked, trusted by the family... He was relied upon, irreplaceable in their eyes, but he was still hired help, and looking across the ranch yard at Nora, he realized what he wanted—to be next to her. Not as a friend. Not as the ranch manager. Not as a secret, either. He wanted to be with her, the man by her side.

There was work to be done, and he was the manager around here, so he turned away to check on the barbecues. Cliff wasn't here anymore to keep everything running smoothly. That responsibility was Easton's now.

From across the yard, he heard Rosie's soft cry. Strange that he should be able to pick out which baby was crying, but he could. The last little while with the girls in his house had attuned him to their schedules and the sound of their whimpers and wails. He glanced over to see Audrey trying to shush the little thing. Nora was feeding Bobbie her bottle, and Riley was with a younger cousin who looked absolutely thrilled to be holding a baby. Kaitlyn took Rosie from Audrey's arms, but Rosie wouldn't be soothed, and she wouldn't take the bottle, either.

"Everything okay, boss?" Tony asked, following the direction of Easton's gaze.

"Yeah, of course."

Easton turned away. This wasn't his job, and he tried to ignore that plaintive cry. She was in good hands—most of the women there had raised babies of their own. But he couldn't cut himself off from Rosie's wail. It wasn't just "some baby," it was Rosie, who normally was happy as long as she was being cuddled.

Why couldn't he just tune this out? It was like Rosie's cry was tugging at him.

Tony had the barbecues under control. He turned and strode across the yard.

Rosie's face was red with the effort of her cries. Her tiny fists pumped the air, and while all logic said that he shouldn't have any more success than Audrey did, he had a feeling that he might.

"Howdy," he said, giving Audrey a disarming smile. "Let me try."

"What?" Audrey looked surprised to be spoken to, let alone that Easton would offer to take the baby from her. "No, I'm fine. Thank you." She turned bodily away from him as if he was some stranger instead of the man who'd been helping to care for these babies for the last couple of weeks.

"Audrey, let him," Nora said from a few paces away.

The older woman reluctantly passed the infant over, and Easton gathered her up in his arms, flipped her onto her back and patted her diapered rump with a few firm pats. Rosie's wails stopped, and she opened her eyes, looking up at him in mild surprise.

"Hey, there," he said quietly. "Miss me?"

Rosie blinked a couple of times and opened her mouth in a tiny yawn.

"Well, I'll be—" Audrey said, her tone chilly. "I don't think he's washed his hands, Nora."

"He's fine," Nora replied. "Rosie likes him."

And she didn't like Audrey—that much was clear. It was a strange relief to have this little girl in his arms again, and to know that she wasn't crying her heart out anymore, either. That irritating tug at his heartstrings had relaxed, and he heaved a sigh.

"That did the trick," Nora said, coming up beside him. "Thanks."

"Yeah, sure." He smiled slightly then put Rosie up on his shoulder. She snuggled into his neck. "Not sure how I'm going to do anything else around here, though."

"Supervise." Nora shot him a grin. "I'm sure Rosie would love the walk around."

So he'd be a cowboy trotting around with a baby in his arms. Somehow that didn't seem so bad. He might not be family, but he was the answer to Rosie's cries, and that resonated deep inside him in a way that he knew would only hurt all the more when this was over.

And his time here at the Carpenter ranch was coming to an end. He'd known that Cliff's death had changed things, but Nora's return home had solidified that in his mind. Easton reached out and tucked a tendril of hair behind Nora's ear. He'd miss her—oh, how he'd miss her. He'd miss these girls, too. But any more time spent at the Carpenter ranch, and he'd never be able to disentangle his heart.

Sometimes a man had to put his future first.

NORA LET ONE of her cousins take Bobbie from her arms, and she glanced back toward Easton. He was walking Rosie around the fence and appeared to be pointing out horses to her. She had foggy memories of being held in her own father's strong arms, her dad sitting her on the top rail of the fence and pointing out the horses. She'd have been three or four at the time, but the similarity still made her heart ache.

Why was it that a man could make an excellent father, and still not be capable of fidelity? What was it her dad had said about Easton? "He's a younger version of myself, Nora. You could do worse."

Daddy, you ruined him for me...

Her father had ruined a lot of things for her, now that his secret was out. He'd broken a part of her foundation.

"He loves the babies," Kaitlyn said, coming up next to her.

"Yeah..." Nora nodded. "They took to him."

She shouldn't have agreed to stay with Easton. She'd been thinking of giving her mother space, but instead she'd gotten herself into an impossible situation—playing house, almost. They weren't a couple, but sharing a bathroom and a kitchen made imagining herself as part of a couple that much easier...

Kaitlyn looked pale and she slid a hand over her stomach.

"You okay?" Nora asked.

"I think the corn's not sitting right."

Was the corn off? That wouldn't be good. But Nora could see several other people munching on butter-drenched corn on the cob, and no one else looked sick.

"Do you want a drink?" Nora asked. "There are cans of ginger ale on the table."

Kaitlyn nodded. "Yeah, I think I'll get one."

Her husband, Brody, was already at the drink table, and Nora watched as her friend tipped her head against Brody's shoulder. He slid an arm around her waist, and Nora couldn't help but feel a stab of envy. Brody handed his wife a can of ginger ale, and Nora didn't miss the way he looked at her. Kaitlyn had it all—the doting husband, the supportive extended family, a home that was ready for kids.

Like the adoptive family in Billings who were anxiously awaiting her decision, she realized bitterly. They were ready for more children. They had it all, too—the home, the marriage, the money, the career… Everything that Nora lacked, that family could give. And family most definitely mattered.

Nora turned back toward her own milling family and ranch hands, who were starting to line up for freshly barbecued sausages and burgers. A family was more than support, it was a library of personal histories. Family never forgot the details, even if you'd rather they did. Rewriting history wasn't possible with a family this size—there was no avoiding the truth.

It was one thing to embrace who you were, but it was that very history that would plague these girls for the rest of their lives in this town. Did she want to raise them and have them move away from her as quickly as possible to get away from the dysfunctional family tensions?

Rosie seemed to have fallen asleep on Easton's

shoulder, and he patted her back idly, chatting with one of the ranch hands.

Babies were simple—diapers, bottles, hugs. It was raising the older versions of these triplets that truly intimidated her. And she couldn't do it alone. Sometimes true love meant hanging on through thick and thin, and other times it meant backing off to allow happiness to come from someone else. As much as she hated to consider it, giving the girls up might be the best choice.

Chapter Thirteen

Rosie slept for a while propped up on Easton's shoulder. The other ranch hands showed him an odd amount of respect with a baby in his arms, and when a couple of guys were getting too noisy, one look from him silenced them.

Clouds had been gathering again after a clear afternoon, and the wind had cooled noticeably. People were gathered around various tables of food, some sitting in lawn chairs and others lounging on blankets. A few ranch hands were sitting on upended firewood as they ate their burgers. The day might stay fair yet, though a smudge of cloud could be seen a few miles west.

"Looks like rain," Tony said, biting into a burger and talking past his food.

"Yeah, maybe," Easton agreed, although for the sake of the corn roast, he hoped not. Rosie pulled her knees up and wriggled. A smell mingled with the scent of barbecued meat. Was that what he thought it was?

Tony looked at the baby in Easton's arms and made a face. "Baby's leaking," he announced.

Easton pulled Rosie away from his chest and gave

her a once-over. The ranch hand was right. A smear had formed by the edge of her diaper, corresponding with that suspicious smell.

"Wow, Rosie," Easton said, and Rosie opened her eyes enough to blink at him before shutting them again. "I'd better bring her back to Nora."

"Good call," Tony agreed.

Easton headed back through the yard where Nora had been earlier, but she was nowhere to be seen now. Neither were the other two babies.

"Nora's inside," Kaitlyn called. She was sipping from a can of pop. He smiled his thanks and headed in the direction of the side door.

He stepped inside and the screen door banged shut behind him. The house was silent, everyone outside with the food, and he paused in the entryway to the kitchen, unsure of what to do.

"Nora?" he called.

Nora looked around the doorway to the living room, and he stopped short when he saw her face. Her eyes were red, and she wiped at her cheek with one hand. She'd been crying.

"You okay?" he asked.

His boots thunked across the kitchen floor, and he emerged into the living room. She wiped at her face again as if trying to hide the evidence.

"Fine," she said quickly. "Just working on diapers."

She wasn't fine—he wasn't blind. Nora had the babies laid out on towels on the floor. She added a third towel when she saw Rosie, and he laid the baby next to her sisters.

"Hey," he said softly. "Nora—"

"I'm fine!" Her voice rose, and he could tell she was fighting back tears. Something had happened—had someone said something? Was there more flack about her dad? Protectiveness simmered deep inside him—he'd deal personally with whoever had caused this. But she didn't say anything else.

Nora unsnapped Riley's onesie and peeled back the tabs on the diaper. He could stand there, or he could help. Easton knelt next to her and started with Rosie's diaper. If nothing else, he could do this. He'd seen Nora do enough diapers that he knew the drill—theoretically, at least.

"Wipes," he said, and she passed them over.

They worked silently for a couple of minutes, and Nora passed him a new sleeper for Rosie.

"I need help with this one," he said. He had Rosie diapered, but the sleeper was going to be tricky. Nora smiled feebly, and gave him a hand with tiny arms and legs that just kept curling back as if she were inside an egg. When the babies were all changed and dressed, Easton and Nora sat on the floor and leaned against the couch. The babies were snuggled up together in front of them. They looked so peaceful—Riley's little fist resting on Bobbie's face, and Rosie making sucking noises as she dozed. These girls had the life right now—anything could be fixed with a diaper change and a nap.

"So what's going on?" Easton asked.

Nora looked toward him for a moment then sighed. "I visited a family that wants to adopt the babies."

The information took a moment to sink in, and when it did, Easton's stomach sank. "You did? When?"

She shrugged weakly. "This morning. They live in Billings—the father is a child psychologist…" She licked her lips. "They can give the girls so much. Financial security, love, good schools, a stay-at-home mom—" Tears misted her eyes again. "More than I can." The last words came out in a whisper.

The thought of these babies going to another family felt wrong—like a betrayal, although he had no right to feel that way. He knew it—this wasn't about him.

"And you're really considering this?" he asked.

"I can't do it alone, Easton. Mom is so hurt by Dad's affair that she can't face doing this with me, and I don't even blame her. You know people are talking about it. It's one thing to deal with what he did, and quite another to face the questions and pitying looks that she'd get constantly with the girls living with her…"

Easton understood, but was that really the end of it? Was there no other way for Nora to keep the girls with her? He knew firsthand how much she loved these babies, and he knew exactly what it would do to her to give them to another family. If he left Hope, at least he'd hold on to the mental image of Nora and these triplets together. Separating them…

"The homestead," he said. "If your father hadn't left it to me, you'd have been able to stay there."

Was he the one standing between her and keeping these girls?

"What if you bought me out?" Easton asked. "Dale suggested that. You could have that house again. It belongs with family anyway. I know your dad was trying to do something nice for me, but if he knew what it would do to you and his granddaughters, he wouldn't have willed it to me. I know that for a fact."

"I can't buy you out." Her voice was tight and she swallowed hard. "If I stay here, I won't be working right away. I can't get into a mortgage."

"Then stay with me." The words surprised him, but this was a solution. He didn't have to leave Hope, did he? They were already staying together quite successfully. He could continue helping out with the girls, and she wouldn't have to worry about rent or anything like that. He could rethink that escape he'd been planning—if she needed him.

"How would that work?" she asked, shaking her head.

"Like it has been." He turned to face her and slipped his arm behind her. "We've been working it so far. I could get used to this. Couldn't you?"

"No." There was a tremor in her voice.

Did she mean that? Was she already finished taking what she needed from him?

"Why not?" he asked, irritated. They'd better just get this out into the open. If she was done with his help, he needed to hear it, because that was the only way he was going to accept this—if she told him straight.

"Because it doesn't solve *us*!" Nora's voice shook and she blinked back tears. "What are we going to do, keep cuddling on the couch, kissing on the porch and live together like a couple? That's *not* a solution, Easton. That's a shortcut to heartbreak, and I'm not doing it. You're a lot like my dad, you know." She swallowed hard. "He said it over and over again—that you're just like he was when he was young. You know what that means to me. It's so hard to trust—"

Yeah, he understood all of that, but in spite of it all, they'd been taking care of those girls together. He wished she could trust him, see deep inside him and recognize the man in there—but apparently some things would never change between them.

Easton leaned closer as her words trailed off, and she met his gaze, her breath catching as he took her lips with his. Her eyes drifted closed and she leaned into his kiss. She was warm and soft, and he moved closer, tugging her into his arms. Why couldn't this work? He'd had reasons of his own up until this moment, but he couldn't seem to think straight when he was with her, and certainly not with his lips moving over hers.

She pulled back and shook her head, her fingers fluttering up to her lips. "We've got to stop that," she breathed.

"Do we?" he asked, catching her gaze and holding it. "Really?"

Because he sure didn't want to. She looked ready to reconsider, and given a chance he'd move in for another kiss, but she moved back.

"Easton, stop it."

That was clear enough. He pulled his hand back.

"I'm not starting something I can't finish." She whispered. "Love you or not—"

And maybe he should appreciate that she wouldn't start up with him if she could foresee herself walking away…but she'd mentioned love and his heart skipped a hopeful beat.

"*Do* you love me?" His voice dropped and he swallowed.

Tears rose in her eyes. "Against my better judgment."

He felt the smile tug at his lips. How long had he waited to hear that confession? How many years had he dreamed of her finally seeing the man he was at heart?

"Because I've loved you for years." He remembered all those years of loving her from afar, being there for her in her tough times and watching her walk away when she pulled it all together again. He could push those memories aside and ignore it in a heated moment when he was so focused on getting closer to her…but what about after the conquest? What about after he had her, and they settled into a routine? She'd never wanted what he could offer before—not for the long-term. His own mother hadn't wanted him, either. He knew better than to start expecting things.

She was vulnerable. He was pushing this, and pressure wouldn't change the end result.

"But I know what you mean," he said gruffly. "I want to short-cut this so badly, but you're right. We should stop."

Tears glistened in her eyes, and he leaned forward and pressed his lips against her forehead. How he longed to kiss those lips again, to forget all the logic and clear thinking, and just melt into her arms. But she was right. Trust was the problem here—she was afraid he'd turn out just like her dad, and he was afraid that she'd walk away when things got tough. There was no point in starting something that would end in him staring at an empty spot in the closet…again. There were only so many times a man could have his heart torn apart in one lifetime, and he was pretty sure he'd already reached his limit.

"So I'm right." Nora swallowed hard. This would be a first—a man admitting that he would likely be unfaithful. But what was she wanting him to do—try to change her mind? She wasn't that easily swayed.

"Not about me cheating," he said, "but I understand why you're scared. I doubt I could convince you that I'm any different. That's an argument I can't win."

Nora's chest felt tight. "It shouldn't be an argument, should it?"

"Probably not." He rubbed a hand over his face, and the gesture brought back memories of the teenage Easton in a flood. He was no kid anymore, and he'd proven that over the last two weeks. This was a man in front of her—a man just like her father.

"Thing is, Nora, I can't offer you the world. I don't have it to give. You're used to a better life than I am, and I'm pretty sure I can't match what you're used to. You're afraid of me turning out like your dad, and you couldn't face that kind of heartbreak. Well, I can't face being walked out on by another woman I love."

Another woman like his mom? For years Nora had watched that sadness swirl inside Easton, and only recently did she discover what had caused it. Now, she blamed his mother, resented her, even. Easton deserved better…and he thought she'd be no different? That hurt.

"Do you really worry about that?"

"Life gets hard," he said quietly. "Really hard. I don't think my mom imagined herself leaving, either, until she did it." He scrubbed a hand through his hair. "And maybe I'm a little bit like her, too. She got out of this town—started fresh where no one knew her past. I get why she'd want that so badly. I've been thinking seriously about doing the same thing."

Easton's words hit her like a blow to the stomach. He would leave? Somehow that hadn't occurred to her as even a possibility, even though she knew other ranchers had been trying to woo him. Easton had been a constant around here. The ranch ran like clockwork because of his professional skills. But he was more than an employee at the ranch—her dad had made sure of that. It was impossible to imagine this place without him. It would be empty here—lonely.

"But you *live* here." It sounded so trite, but she couldn't articulate the depth of her feelings about this. This was his home—over the years he'd become an integral part of *her* home, and she'd taken his presence here entirely for granted. Could he really just walk away?

She rose to her feet, walked toward the window then turned back. He stood up, too, and they stared at each other for a few beats. Easton nodded a few times as if coming to a conclusion.

"I wanted to sell you the house—it would give me money for a new start—but I'm used to roughing it.

I'll sign the house back over to you. I'll give your mom my written notice tomorrow."

Anger writhed against the wall of sadness, and she strode back over and punched him solidly in the chest. "You're seriously just going to leave?" she demanded. "Just like that?"

"I can't do this!" His voice raised and he stopped, shutting his eyes for a moment. Then he moderated his tone. "Nora, I'm *not* doing this anymore. I'm not sitting here, loving you, and not having anything more. We both know why it can't work, and you're right—playing house isn't going to take the place of a real, honest commitment. I don't want to just see what happens—I want a family that I can claim as mine. Call that old-fashioned if you want, but it's what I want. And I know myself—I'm not going to get over you that easily. You don't love a girl for over a decade and just bounce back." He swallowed hard. "I never have."

He was right—just like when they were teens, she wanted too much. She wanted him to be there, her support, her confidant. If the last couple of weeks had taught her anything, it was that skirting that line between friendship and more was harder than she'd imagined. He wasn't the only one who sailed past "just friends" in a vulnerable moment. It wasn't fair to expect him to keep trying to toe the line, and she knew that, but the thought of losing him completely…well, that tore at her heart. Their balance wasn't a long-term solution.

He deserved a full life. He deserved a family of

his own. Who was she to stand between him and his happiness?

"I'm going to miss you." Her chin trembled, and she struggled to maintain control.

"Me, too. But at least I'll have made it possible for you to keep the girls. I think it's what your dad would have wanted."

Outside, lightning flashed and there was a boom overhead. Rain spattered against the living room window. Easton put his hat on just as the kitchen door opened and people came pouring inside. He held her gaze for a moment, those dark eyes swimming with regret. Then he turned and walked away as the first wave of aunts and cousins flooded, laughing, into the living room.

He'd sign the house back over to her. All would be balanced again, and she'd have a home to raise the girls. She'd have the homestead in her name—her family's history back where it belonged. It wouldn't solve everything, but it was a good start. Yet despite all she would gain, she was losing the man she'd loved against all her better judgment. Pain was the cost of having loved, but the price of saying goodbye to Easton was almost more than her heart could bear.

Chapter Fourteen

Easton stood in his kitchen, the coffeepot percolating on the stove next to him. He felt gutted, scraped out. His throat felt as raw as if he'd cried, although he hadn't shed any tears. He'd been trying to avoid this kind of pain by not starting up with her, but that hadn't exactly worked, had it? He was alone—Nora had stayed at her mother's house to weather out the storm, but he didn't get that luxury. He still had a job to do, and it only got harder during inclement weather.

Even with Nora gone, there were reminders of her, from the baby chairs lined up across the kitchen table, to the soft feminine scent that lingered. What was that—soap, shampoo, just her? He couldn't tell, but he liked it. He'd never had a woman living with him before. Not since his mother, at least, and he wished he didn't know how soothing a voice filtering through the floorboards could be, or how nice a hallway could smell while the steam from a shower seeped through the crack under the door.

Easton had been serious when he said he'd sign the house over to her. He couldn't keep this land and still like himself. He could let Nora live in this house and keep it in his name, but even that felt wrong. It should be hers—completely hers.

The bird-patterned curtains billowed in the wind that whistled through the open window, and he heaved it shut. From the very beginning he'd known that she belonged here, and that was why he'd never been able to take down those curtains. The house had a soul, and it was time for him to stop making another family his own, and start fresh.

The coffee was done percolating, and he flicked off the stove. He'd let his brew sit until he got back. He needed to double-check that all the horses were inside the barn, check the locks for the night and then he could call it a day. Tomorrow he'd give his notice. It was probably better to do this as quickly as possible.

Thunder crashed outside, and it shook the house hard enough for some silverware to rattle in the sink. He headed to the mudroom and grabbed his hat and an oil slicker.

He'd miss this house, this family and its connection to the only woman he'd ever loved. Until he left, however, he had a job to do, and they could count on him to be professional. It was all he had left.

NORA STOOD BY the window, watching the rain come down in sheets. The storm had raged for hours now without any respite—the savagery of the weather matching her mood. Wind whipped through the trees, tearing at the leaves and whistling ominously. A crack, a boom and then a flash of lightning lit up the sky. She glanced back to the couch where the babies lay in their usual row, sound asleep and oblivious to nature's tantrum. Dina sat in a rocking chair next to the couch, and when the lightning flashed, she'd instinctively put a hand out toward them.

"Why don't you look happier, Nora?" her mother asked quietly.

Nora came back to the couch and bent down to push a soother back into Bobbie's mouth.

"I told you—he's leaving."

"But you said that he's signing the house back over to you," her mother said. "You can raise the girls. You wanted that…"

"I'm still wondering if that's the right choice." Nora ran a finger down Bobbie's silken cheek. "I want it, but with all of the gossip here…" She pulled her hand back and straightened. "I came home for you, Mom. Not for Aunt Audrey, or Uncle Dale, or anyone else. I came for *you*."

"I know. And that was the right thing to do—"

"Except in this—" Nora bit back the rest. It was wrong to push this—to plead for more. But when she came home, it was because it was the only way she could handle all of this. She needed her mother's support, and if raising the girls meant she'd be isolated in that little house, trying to explain away people's attitudes to little girls with tender hearts, then keeping them would still be a mistake.

"It's all been a shock to me," Dina said quietly. "The love of my life cheated on me, and I didn't even get the chance to scream at him." Tears misted her eyes, and

she sighed. "That's the thing that I'm angriest about—
he didn't give me the chance. I needed to deal with this
whole mess with him, not *after* him." She reached out
and touched Rosie's tiny, bare foot. "I just needed some
time, sweetheart."

"Has anything changed?" Nora asked cautiously.

"I suppose," her mother said. "You have no idea
how much I appreciate you giving me space in my own
house, Nora. I did some crying and screaming into
my pillow. I've had my time to argue with your dad in
my head, play out on all the different scenarios, but at
the end of it all, I come to one thing—I love him. Not
past tense. I still do. I always will. I just don't think I
can be Grandma."

Anything less than Grandma wasn't good enough—
it was too distant to be any use. They were back to
where they'd been all along—

"I think I'd be Nana," Dina said. "I've always thought
I'd be a good Nana."

Nora blinked, her heart speeding up. "Nana?"

"Does it suit me?" her mother asked uncertainly.
"Or is that too old-sounding?"

Nora wrapped her arms around her mom and swallowed against the emotion in her throat.

"It's perfect, Mom."

Dina squeezed Nora's hand and looked up into her
daughter's face. "If your dad had been brave enough
to tell me the truth, I'd have been angry—that's true.
I'd have screamed and cried and stomped out for as
long as I needed to. But after we worked through all
of that, I'd have stood by him." Her chin trembled with

emotion. "I'd have been a stepmom to Mia. He didn't give me the chance."

And how different Nora's childhood would have been! She'd have had a sister—but whether or not they'd have been able to like each other at that stage was up for debate. She'd have known the worst, and that would have been easier in some ways. But it wouldn't change the fact that she'd never quite trust that a man could stay faithful.

"I don't think I'd be that noble myself," Nora said. "When Dad cheated on you, he broke more than your trust, he broke *mine*. I thought he was the world, Mom. I really did. I thought if I could find a man like my dad, I'd be happy ever after. But that's no guarantee, is it? Because even Dad couldn't stay faithful."

"And you're afraid that Easton wouldn't be faithful, either," her mother concluded.

Nora was silent, and her mother shot her a rueful smile.

"I still know you better than you think. You love him."

Nora tried to swallow the lump in her throat. "It's so stupid…"

"No, it isn't," her mother replied. "He's loved you for years. In the last few years your dad hoped that you'd—"

"My dad doesn't get a vote!" Nora snapped.

Her mother rose to her feet and went to the sideboard. She picked up the small framed photo that Nora had brought from the old farmhouse. She looked at the photo for a few moments then handed it over to Nora.

"Did you ever hear the story about that tractor?" Dina asked.

"No, I don't think so."

"This picture reminded me of it because it probably happened at about this point in their marriage, before the kids. This picture is in the summer, but the winters could be really harsh. One winter, your great-grandfather had gone out to check on the cows. Their breath could freeze over their noses, even in the barn. So he went out in a blizzard to do his check. Anyway, he didn't come back, and your great-grandmother waited and waited. She got worried—her husband had his routines and she knew something had gone wrong. So she bundled up and went after him. She found him in the barn, but he was knocked out cold underneath the tractor. No one knows what happened exactly, but he must have slipped on some ice, the tractor had rolled and he was pinned. You see the size of her in that photo—"

Nora looked down at the slim, light-haired woman, leaning up against the wheel of that tractor.

"The story goes," her mother went on, "that she picked up that tractor herself, hoisted it off her husband and carried him from the barn back to the house. She saved his life that day."

"Is it true?" Nora asked. She hardly looked big enough for those kinds of heroics.

Her mother shrugged. "It's family lore. You can decide if you believe it. But the point I'm trying to make is that when you choose a man, you're not trusting in his strength alone. You bring strength to the table, too. Your great-grandfather couldn't have run that dairy without her, and he'd surely have died that night if she hadn't gone after him. So yes, men can make mistakes. They can let you down. They can break your heart. Heck, they can even die on you. But you aren't passive in all of this, and you aren't putting your faith in him alone." Her mother fiddled with the wedding ring on her finger. "You're strong, Nora. And you're smart. You're a force to be reckoned with. You aren't trusting in a fallible man, you're trusting in what the two of you are together. Don't underestimate what you bring to the relationship."

Nora turned back to the window, her heart hammering in her chest. She had no control over the future, and she had no guarantee against heartbreak. But she knew what she felt for Easton, and she knew what he felt for her. She'd felt the strength of his feelings when he held her in his arms, and if she was only trusting emotion alone...

Easton had told her that he wasn't sure she could handle a life with him—the ups and downs, the uncertainties. But she knew in the depth of her heart that she could. She could weather any storm with Easton, if she knew that they were weathering it together. She could be his strength, just as much as he could be hers.

But he was leaving—and that realization shook her to the core.

"Mom, I need to talk to him," Nora said, turning to face her mother. She looked toward the babies then back out at the storm.

"I'll stay with the girls," her mother said. "Go."

Nora went through the kitchen to the mudroom,

grabbed a hat from a peg and snatched up her mother's oil slicker. She needed to talk to him…there was more to say. He might still leave, but at least she'd have said it all before he did.

Chapter Fifteen

Nora slammed the door to the old homestead behind her and shook off her rain slicker. She'd barely been able to make out the road through the deluge on her windshield, and she'd nearly gone off the road a few times, but she'd made it all right. There were lights on in the kitchen.

"Easton?" she called.

Silence. She glanced around the kitchen and saw nothing amiss. She went over to the stove and lifted the lid of the coffeepot—it was completely full, but only barely warm. She knew his routine. He percolated his coffee then left it to cool a little while he did his last rounds, checking locks and whatnot. If the coffee was nearly cold, then he'd been gone a long time.

Thunder rumbled again, a pause then a mighty crack as the room lit up in a momentary blinding display. She looked out the window as the realization dawned on her. Easton was out there somewhere, and if there wasn't a problem, he'd have been back long ago. The other ranch hands were supposed to have done the last of the work, and he was only doing the last check. Even in a winter storm, it shouldn't take this long.

Nora pulled her cell phone out of her pocket and dialed his number. It rang, but there was no reply. Obviously not—he'd be crazy to pick up a call in that downpour, if he even heard it. Should she stay a little longer and wait? Accidents happened in storms, and a mental image of that tractor in the black-and-white photo rose in her mind. It was silly, maybe, but she'd feel better if she found him.

She slipped back into the rain slicker and pushed her hat back onto her head. She opened the door and had to shoulder it to beat back the wind. Rain swamped her as she pushed through the blinding torrent. It took twice as long to get to her truck, and when she was finally creeping down the road toward the barn, she could barely see a thing past her swishing wipers. She knew his circuit ended with the barn, so she'd try there.

The wind changed direction momentarily, and she could see movement in the horse corral. Horses couldn't possibly still be outside, could they? She pulled up next to the barn and tried to see through the downpour, but couldn't make anything out. She'd have to check in person. She pulled her coat up around her neck—it wasn't going to do much good, but it was something—then hopped back out into the driving rain.

"He's fine," she muttered to herself, preparing to come across him dry and safe in the barn, but through the howl of the wind, she caught the terrified whinny of a horse.

Had she heard that right? Her boots slipped in the

mud as she made her way around the side of the barn, rain pounding against her so that she had to keep her eyes shut until she made it to the gate to the corral. She shielded her eyes, and in a flash of lightning, she saw him. He was holding a lead rope, and Scarlet had reared up on her hind legs, pawing the air in fright. As the mare came down, she didn't see the point of contact, but Easton crumpled.

Nora fumbled with the latch, but soon she was through. She slipped and slid through the mud, and grabbed the lead rope again, pulling Scarlet closer.

"Easton!" she gasped.

He crawled farther away, one arm tucked around his side. He'd need medical attention tonight after that kick, but first the horse had to be calmed. She fumbled with the buttons of her coat, and as she tried to take it off, Scarlet reared again. Nora jumped back and tore the coat from her body at the same time. A blast of cold rain hit her, but she was too focused to shiver. She caught the lead rope again, and when the horse came down, she whipped the coat over the mare's head. The horse whinnied in fear, but didn't rear again. Without the lightning to spook her, she'd be able to find her calm again.

Nora gulped in deep breaths of humid air and murmured softly as she led Scarlet toward the barn door. Easton pushed himself to his feet and followed. His face was ashen as he came into the light of the barn, and he hunched forward with a grimace.

"You okay?" she asked.

"Sure." That was a lie, because he leaned back against the wall, wincing. "Just let me rest a second."

EVERY BREATH LANCED through Easton's side, and he breathed as shallowly as possible as he watched Nora get Scarlet settled in her stall. He'd been impressed—she'd known exactly what to do. If she hadn't shown up when she did, Scarlet might have been seriously hurt. Let alone him...

Nora locked the stall and headed in his direction. He tried to straighten a little more, look slightly less pathetic, but he wasn't sure it worked. She hauled a stool over to him and helped him sink down onto it. That made things easier, but he still didn't like being the winded one.

"Let me see." She eased his slicker off his shoulders and he grimaced as he straightened. Then her fingers deftly undid the front buttons of his shirt and she pulled it aside to reveal purple and red welts across his side. She ran cool fingers over his skin and when she reached his ribs, he let out a grunt of pain.

"Broken," she confirmed.

"Why were you out here?" he breathed.

"Your coffee was cold," she said irritably. "You never let your coffee get cold."

She knew him better than he thought, and he was grateful that she'd come after him. She wasn't calming down, though. Her eyes snapped fire and she took a step back.

"You know as well as I do that you're not supposed to be working with spooked animals alone. That's a safety issue! You could have been killed, you know! A good kick to the head, and it could have been over for you!"

"Had to make a choice," he said, pushing himself up against the pain. He caught her hand as she went to touch the spot again. "Nora, I'm fine."

"You are *not* fine!" Tears welled up in her eyes, and the blood drained from her face. He squeezed her hand and felt her trembling.

"Stop." He tugged her against his other side, but the pain was nearly unbearable.

"I'm hurting you." She pulled back.

"Just a bit." But yeah, maybe less squeezing. He attempted to adjust his position. She was watching him, and it was more than sympathy in those cloudy eyes. "What?" he asked.

She pushed a wet strand of hair out of her face. "I had to ask you to stay."

This only made it harder. They'd been over this already.

"Nora, I can't just be your—"

She moved in closer, her mouth a breath away from his, and the words evaporated on his tongue. Then she closed the distance. His body immediately responded to her, but when he leaned into the kiss, he was stopped by that slice of pain.

"Nora, you gotta stop doing that to me," he said with a low laugh. "A guy's liable to get the wrong idea."

"Please stay," she whispered.

"I thought we talked about this." Did they have to rehash this again to convince themselves that this was folly? It wasn't a matter of not wanting her—he wanted her so much it would probably scandalize her. But if he let himself go, really let himself love her with all the passion that he kept sealed away inside him, he wouldn't be able to turn it off when she couldn't face the hard stuff. That would be a heartbreak that would never heal. What man walked into that willingly?

"My mom told me something tonight that made a whole lot of sense. She said that when you choose a man, you aren't just putting your faith in his strength and his character, you're choosing what the two of you are together. I'm scared, I'll admit that, but I'm no wallflower, either. Together, you and I are pretty tough, Easton. It isn't just you—it's who you are when you're with me. And who I am when I'm with you. And I think—" She blushed slightly then looked down. "I think we're something special when we're together."

He reached out and caught her hand, easing her closer until he could put his arm around her waist. He held her there, his mind spinning. She'd just braved the worst storm in a decade because his coffee was cold. Obviously, he'd misjudged how tough she was. She'd come after him and hauled a spooked horse away from him, to boot.

"I'm not staying here for friendship," he clarified. "I'll lay it out for you. If I stay, I want to get married and raise those girls together. I want the whole package, Nora. Three kids. Mr. and Mrs. Maybe-More-Kids-Later-On."

Her gaze flicked up to meet his—steady, constant.

"And I can't offer much money. Heck, I work for

your mom. I might move on to another ranch—depends on the future. If you take me, you take me in the good times and the bad. But I'll work my hardest to keep those times good…" His voice caught. Would she accept him when she really thought it through? He was putting it all on the line—everything he had to offer. He wasn't holding anything up his sleeve.

"You want to raise the girls with me?" she asked. "You really do? Because there is no halfway with three kids, Easton."

"I'm not offering halfway," he said, running his work-roughened hands over her smooth ones. "I know what it's like to grow up under a shadow. My family has a stigma around here, so I get it. I don't ever want those girls to feel like they were less than wanted. I want to raise them together, love them like crazy and teach them how to let stupid comments roll off their backs. I love you, Nora. I want to marry you, and I want to be the only daddy those girls ever know. So if you're serious about this—if you're willing to be something with me, then I want to be married. What do you say?"

"I say yes." Her eyes sparkled with unshed tears and she nodded.

It took him a moment to register her words, but when he did, he pulled her into a kiss until he couldn't take the pain anymore. He let out a soft moan and she eased out of his arms.

"Let's go," she said, helping him to stand. "You need a doctor."

"I'll be fine," he muttered.

"Are you going to try to fight me?" she asked incredulously. "Because if you can stand up straight, I'll let you be."

He smiled ruefully. "Never mind." He allowed her to guide him to the door. The wind had died down and it was just rain now, thunder rumbling in the distance.

"I want to marry you just as soon as you can find a dress you like," he said with a low laugh. "I hope you shop fast."

After all these years of holding himself back, he was never going to get tired of pulling that beautiful woman into his arms. She was right—they were better together, they were tougher together and they were just what those girls needed around here. The triplets might have been born Hamptons, but they'd be the Ross kids, and no one would ever make them feel less than the beautiful gifts that they were. Their dad would make sure of it.

Epilogue

On a chilly autumn morning, as rain pattered down on the little church in downtown Hope, Nora stood in front of a full-length mirror willing her heartbeat to calm. The veil blurred her vision as she regarded her reflection. She wore a dress of clinging satin cream that spread into a rippling train behind her. The veil was simple, attached to a jeweled tiara that sat on her golden waves. She spread her hands over her fluttering stomach, the engagement ring glittering in the low light.

She was getting married this morning… She'd become Mrs. Nora Ross.

The door opened and Kaitlyn slipped inside the room. She wore an empire waist bridesmaid dress of mint green, and Nora was glad she'd chosen such a forgiving cut now that Kaitlyn's belly had started to grow. After the nausea at the corn roast, Kaitlyn had disbelievingly taken another pregnancy test… She was five months along now and glowing with the new life she carried.

"Are the girls okay?" Nora asked.

"They're all asleep," Kaitlyn reassured her. "And the bottles are ready. They'll be fine. Are you ready?"

"I think so." Nora shot her friend a nervous smile.

"Easton told me to give you this—" Kaitlyn handed her a black velvet box, and Nora looked down at it in surprise.

"Was I supposed to buy him something?" she whispered.

"Oh, stop," Kaitlyn laughed. "Just open it."

Nora pried open the clamshell. Inside was a white gold charm bracelet. She lifted it out of the box, running her fingers over the delicate charms. There were three pink crystal pairs of booties, and on either side of them were two silver halves of a heart. A lump rose in her throat.

"It's us…" she whispered.

At the clasp there was a tiny silver horseshoe— luck. But she didn't need luck. Today they'd confirm their promises in front of friends and family, but these were words Easton had already murmured to her that morning.

I'm going to love you every day, Nora. I'm going to tell you the truth always. I'm going to stand by your side whatever comes at us. I'm yours.

Kaitlyn helped her to put the bracelet on, and as she looked down at the sparkle on her wrist, the old organ's music swelled from the sanctuary where everyone was waiting. Easton was at the front of that church, and imagining him up there, all her nervous jitters melted away.

I'm going to love you every day, Easton. I'm going to tell you the truth always…

These weren't hard promises to keep—they were

simply putting into words what was already there. Today she was marrying her best friend.

"Okay," Nora said, gathering up her train. "I'm ready."

* * * * *

Don't miss the next book in Patricia Johns's
HOPE, MONTANA miniseries,
coming in August 2017 from
Harlequin Western Romance.

And check out previous books in the miniseries:
SAFE IN THE LAWMAN'S ARMS
HER STUBBORN COWBOY
THE COWBOY'S CHRISTMAS BRIDE
THE COWBOY'S VALENTINE BRIDE

Get 2 Free Books,

♦HARLEQUIN® ~Western ~Romance

Plus 2 Free Gifts —
just for trying the
Reader Service!

SPECIAL EXCERPT FROM

⬢ HARLEQUIN®

Western Romance

Becca Johnston doesn't need a distraction like her new tenant, rugged rodeo champ Sawyer McCall. But having a good man around the house means so much to her young son and she's definitely enjoying the handsome cowboy's attention...

Read on for a sneak preview of
THE COWBOY UPSTAIRS,
the next book in Tanya Michaels's
***CUPID'S BOW, TEXAS** series.*

"Mr. Sawyer, do you like pizza?"

"As a matter of fact, I love it."

"Then you should—"

"Marc! Scoot."

"—have dinner with us."

Becca bit back a groan.

"Well," he said as the door clattered shut, "at least one of you likes me."

Now that he was on the step just below her, she could see his eyes were green, flecked with gold, and she hated herself for noticing. "So is Sawyer your first name or last?"

"First. Sawyer McCall." He extended a hand. "Pleasure to meet you. Officially."

Her fingers brushed over his in something too brief to qualify as a handshake before she pulled away. "Becca Johnston. What are you doing here?"

"I need a place to stay."

She bit the inside of her lip. When she'd had the bright idea to rent out her attic, she certainly hadn't considered giving the key to a smug, sexy stranger.

"I can pay up front. Cash. And I can give you a list of references to assure you I'm not some whack job."

"Mr. McCall, I really don't think—"

The screen door banged open and a mini tornado gusted across the porch in the form of her son. "You're still here! Are you staying for pizza? Mama, can I show him my space cowboys and robot horses?"

Becca studied her son's eager face and tried to recall the last time she'd seen him look so purely happy. "Mr. McCall and I aren't finished talking yet, champ. Why don't you go set the table for three?"

Marc disappeared back inside as quickly as he'd come.

She took a deep breath. "The attic apartment has its own back stair entrance and a private bathroom. Whoever I rent the room to is welcome to join Marc and I for meals—but, in exchange, I was hoping to find someone with a bit of child-care experience. Occasional babysitting in trade for my cooking."

He shrugged. "Sounds reasonable."

"Then, assuming your references check out, you've got a deal, Mr. McCall."

His grin, boldly triumphant and male, sent tiny shivers up her arms. "When do I get to see my room?"

Don't miss THE COWBOY UPSTAIRS
by Tanya Michaels, available May 2017 wherever
Harlequin® Western Romance
books and ebooks are sold.

www.Harlequin.com